CVC

CVC

Carter V. Cooper

SHORT FICTION ANTHOLOGY SERIES

BOOK TWO

SELECTED BY, AND WITH A PREFACE BY

Gloria Vanderbilt

EXILE
editions

Library and Archives Canada Cataloguing in Publication

CVC : Carter V. Cooper short fiction anthology series : book two / edited by Gloria Vanderbilt

(CVC : Carter V. Cooper short fiction anthology series ; bk. 2)
ISBN 978-1-55096-294-9

1. Short stories, Canadian (English). 2. Canadian fiction (English)--21st century. I. Vanderbilt, Gloria, 1924- II. Series: Carter V. Cooper short fiction anthology series ; bk. 2

PS8329.1.C833 2012   C813'.010806   C2012-903063-5

Published by Exile Editions Ltd ~ www.ExileEditions.com
144483 Southgate Road 14 – GD, Holstein, Ontario, N0G 2A0
Printed and Bound in Canada in 2012

The publisher would like to acknowledge the financial support of the Canada Council for the Arts, the Government of Canada through the Canada Book Fund (CBF), the Ontario Arts Council, and the Ontario Media Development Corporation, for our publishing activities.

Canadian Sales: The Canadian Manda Group, 165 Dufferin Street,
Toronto ON M6K 3H6   www.mandagroup.com   416 516 0911

North American and international Distribution, and U.S. Sales:
Independent Publishers Group, 814 North Franklin Street,
Chicago IL 60610   www.ipgbook.com   toll free: 1 800 888 4741

In memory of

Carter V. Cooper

CVC
BOOK TWO

PREFACE

This annual short fiction competition is open to all Canadian writers, with two prizes awarded: $3,000 for the best story by an emerging writer, and $2,000 for the best story by a writer at any point of her/his career. Hundreds of stories were received in 2011–12, and from the 12 that eventually were shortlisted, I selected the winners, being those that most appealed to me, as a writer, as a reader, and as a lover of the written word on paper. And, like last year, I simply could not choose only two... so have added a second $2,000 prize. I am proud and thrilled that all these wonderful writers are presented in the *CVC Anthology–Book Two,* a special edition published in memory of my son, Carter V. Cooper. About the winners, I have this to say... Christine Miscione: I greatly admire the pared-down writing of "Skin, Just." It hits gut bone. A haunting story, truly amazing. Not a word amiss. I kept thinking about it long after my reading. And still do. Leon Rooke: I was mesmerized by the cantilevered complexities of "Here Comes Henrietta Armani." The unexpected turns it takes, raising a maze of contradicting questions. The conclusion – brilliant – mysterious – perfect. Seán Virgo: I love the fairy tale quality of "Gramarye," turning that which is real into that which is unreal and by doing so merging both into *the* only reality. A magical story beautifully told.

And I want to give a big *Thank You* to the readers who adjudicated this competition: Lawrence Jeffery, Jerry Tutunjian, MT Kelly, and Barry Callaghan... all who have played their own special roles in the development and support of emerging writers.

Gloria Vanderbilt
May, 2012

Christine Miscione

SKIN, JUST

Gum on the sidewalk, and all she can see are moles mis-shapen, moles deadly. Layers of tar covering potholes are moles too, tar on every street, melanoma in every city. And polka-dot bathing suits! And specks on shower tiles! Knots on floorboards, bruises on banana skins, rot in apples, soy-sauce drips left over on tables and the arms of strangers, their tank-topped backs, their mini-skirted legs where skin shines through: moleless, moleful, abnormal, normal, happy.

Happy Moles is the name of a band she imagined starting with her next-door neighbour Petey and his younger sister Tessa. The three of them could take photos of their moles and magnify them on T-shirts. Wear them to every gig. Sell some after the show with their signatures underneath: *Wear our moles with pride.* Except Tessa didn't have any moles. She was clear as a cup of water. She was so see-through you could see through to her veins, her bones, joints oiled and colon cancer screening made easy.

Patient demands assistance immediately, demands biopsy of mole. Mole approximately 5mm, but hard to discern. Sample covered in blood.

It was growing down there for a long time. She saw it day after day, and the colour became angry. At first it was only a little baby speck, full of exuberance, ready for life. These were the happy days, when Happy Moles, the band, was a possibility. But then: slowly, itty-bitty slowly, itty-bitty baby mole began to get greedy. Wanted fame! Wanted to rock the calf right out of an auditorium with hundreds of screaming fans!—

But it wasn't to be.

And then ANGER, crawling anger. Anger slowly turning to multifarious shades of dark. Mole becoming monochrome. Sullen. Mole brooding in its epidermal throne, sinking lower and lower into layers of flesh, lower into dermis, then hypodermis where it grew manic and uncontrollable.

The growing wouldn't stop.

Wild aberrations, crazed mounds of melanocytes in skin's pigmental, skin overfloweth, her cup overflowing with showers of melanoma sparkles. All dangerous hues! All mutations in sacs of jelly mounds of mole on her calf and chest and down to the base of her spine, where moles congregated to praise our Lord Jesus Christ, save her. Save her.

But sadly, nothing could be saved. Not an inch or a centimetre. Not the skin protecting, skin holding in. Not the layers of billowy cauliflower florets bulbous in her brain, where thoughts began, where meat was turned to neural passages long ago during Neanderthal times. This is evolution: Blue eyes. Fair skin. Deranged cells. Abysmal passages in neuroland. This is evolution: Skin cells replicating infinity. Skin cells never stopping. Skin cells' immortal magic.

Until one day she couldn't take it anymore. Squatting in her bedroom. Staring at her calf, at her mole growing crazy – SHE COULD NOT TAKE IT ANYMORE. How much can be encapsulated in that phrase? – She, a pronoun. Could, separated from Not. Could, Not. Could, a verb of possibility. Not, the destroyer. Not destroys could's possibility, as though errant pigment destroys She. Or Her. Take, a verb. It, a pronoun. Anymore, a state of being. Wrapped together: a phrase leading to action, leads to slicing opening skin and digging out the darkness.

Because she just couldn't take it anymore: on her calf, on her calf, her calf. Just couldn't take it anymore on her calf, so she knifed it out of there. Dug like an excavation. Messy like a construction sight. Blood everywhere like menstruation, and she just couldn't take it anymore, so she rushed to the doctor's. Demanded care. Demanded more action. "Doctor, Doctor, here's my mole. Look at my mole. Examine my mole, NOW! I have cancer. I have cancer in my mole in my hand and I need treatment immediately."

Patient presents with mole. Patient presents with calf mole in her hand. Cut-out and in her hand.

It was the gasoline spill on the pavement outside her house. It was the way gasoline turns normal tar dark and irregular. It was how Tessa's molelessness destroyed Happy Moles, made her own skin seem speckled and malignant, made everything cancerous, cancer-filled, moles full of cancer. It was the way the R.O.M. sprouted its own side growth, its jagged tumour, darkly pigmented zigzag malignancy sticking right out the fucking top and down the side while she was walking Bloor St. and couldn't take it anymore.

Patient slips in and out of consciousness. Post-traumatic stress and blood loss from "biopsy." Patient refuses treatment, refuses sedatives. Patient wants mole tested.

And then mole from calf in hand, mole in hand in front of doctor. Doctor takes mole, puts mole in bag. Doctor packages mole for laboratorial assessment.

Patient's mole sent to laboratory. Advised patient to seek emergency counselling. Advised patient to take sedatives. Patient refused. Will return when results are received.

And then waiting. Long stretch of waiting. Days and weeks of waiting. Heaving in her upstairs bedroom, hyperventilating. Reaching internet limits of skin cancer research. Scouring website after website, and then back to the beginning, first website first, then return to the second. Everyday the same cyber circuit, the same heaving in her upstairs bedroom. And she doesn't eat. She doesn't sleep. Fungus grows on food: pancake tumours, floret moulds. Fungus grows on her mole hole, infection everywhere, and she can't bear to look at it. She just can't. And now a big open sore fringed with pus. And now a hole where a mole used to be. And she's waiting, moulding and waiting, moulding and waiting—

Until one day it comes.

A twinkling ring. A call from a receptionist. A soft-spoken charm through the phone earpiece: "Come in immediately, Dr. Urbanstein wants to see you. Your test results are in."

And then such hurry hurry. Dirty clothes thrown over dirty body, thrown into a taxicab speeding down College St – "Hurry, please, HURRY... Can't you go a little faster? I really have to get there NOW" – And jeans rub against calf hole, rubbing dirty bacteria into calf hole while taxicab swerves around cars, flies forward, quick left, left again, hands gripping seat cushion near calf hole, hole leaky, bacterial, hole thrown left and right, cab turns, turns again and comes to a complete stop. Then: a money exchange. A door slam. The tap tap tap of feet hurrying across concrete, feet into a doorway.

"Clara Williamson... Yes, here to see Dr. Urbanstein. Yes, I received a call this morning... Ok, thank you—"

Feet tapping in a waiting room is not so unusual. Every patient taps something, fiddles something else, picks at other things while anxiously awaiting their

turn. Flipping through sticky magazines isn't so unusual either – pick off crumbs on page seventeen; look
at celebrity photos on page twenty-two; skim facts
about silk-lined pillowcases and titillating meatloaf. But
leaking holes on carpeted ground in a waiting room is
irregular. Taxicab excitement tore it open again, blood
dripping into jean fabric, and now it trickle-trickles on
the floor.

Okay, okay, so she's got an open wound. Okay, so
it's leaking everywhere, staining, stinking, but at least
her results are in. At least she can be told what she could
not know about her own body. At least the doctor can
put it all on the table and tell her how much longer she
has to live.

*Patient looks skeletal, infection in her right calf where
7mm mutilation occurred. Antibiotics prescribed. Patient
self-describes as anxious and psychotic. Confirms she has
not eaten in at least six days.*

Cut to the chase, Doctor. She's not here to talk
about her health. She doesn't care about infection. She
doesn't want your antibacterials, your food suggestions,
your sedation medications to relieve the stress of sitting
here waiting for you to tell her the fucking results. Just
give them to her. Tell her what her skin cells said. Tell
her how much longer. Tell her what her mole was!

Negative.

Test results are negative; skin pigments are negating
cancerous undertones, negating inter-body travel to

different regions for fun in the sun and relaxation. But that can't be possible! – Can that be possible? Is it possible for skin cells, angry and black, to be jolly jubilee? Did she cut her mole, desecrate her calf, let infection seep for eight days all for NOTHING?

Patient seems upset at results. Patient bangs hand on forehead continuously. Eventually forced her hand onto her lap. Appears patient has violence and anger-management issues. Prescribed several medications listed below and six days of antibiotics to clear infection. Patient is discharged from clinic.

Tight grip on her antibacterial prescription. Fingers clasping antipsychotics, anti-anxieties, sedatives, sleeping pills. Five slips of prescriptions in her hand, she marches out of the doctor's office, out onto the concrete, out into the sun, sun burning her eyelids, and there's a wrenching pain in her gut, fingers twisting her spleen and stomach into happy organ animals, insides burning like eyelids. All for nothing. All for nothing! Ruined – body RUINED – all for nothing.

Then: five days of antibioticals, pus slurps back to origin, blood crusts into a convex dome, blackens, misshapes. Every day her mantra: All for nothing, ALL FOR NOTHING. Five days of nausea, puke in the bathroom, the kitchen, lethargy on her bed. She can barely get up. Antibiotics suck the life force out of people. But she wouldn't move anyway, even if she felt perfectly fine, even if the doctor assured her she'd live for another forty years. Because she can't bear to look in the mirror and face herself, what she did, how she self-mutilated for no particular reason. Wasn't cancer. Not melanoma. Not basilique or squirmish.

And, sure, the mole hole starts to heal. No more infection or open wound. Instead: a concave dip, right where the dig happened. An irreversible hole where her mole used to be. And, sure, she's healthy, cancer-free, should be rejoicing, should be out dancing in the streets, living life again…

But all she can do is sit on her bed. Her calf-dip killing her. She can't take it, just can't bear to look at it, and everywhere – EVERYWHERE! – holes dip, acne pits, the dip in the sidewalk outside her house, the blemishes of Christie Pits. She throws herself onto her bed and imagines the multitudes of dips and pits that surround her, doesn't want to face the world. Moves inward, into the centre, begins to fetal curl, but her bed dips. And her pillow dips. And she slams her fist onto the mattress making an itty-bitty pit. She just can't escape the pits and dips, the highs and lows. She just can't hide from holes and concavity. Moles and convexity. Skin is everywhere, surfaces everywhere, surfaces and skins ready to dip and valley, pit and dale, normal, abnormal, happy. And so it goes. She sighs, curls inward, fetal curl until she's nothing but a ball. A mole. A small growth of otherwise benign skin.

Leon Rooke

HERE COMES HENRIETTA ARMANI

A. Three One-Sentence "Once upon a Time" Henrietta Armani Stories.

1. It came to Henrietta Armani, once upon a time, that she was not the same person Henrietta Armani had been, once upon a time.

2. The sound of two hands clapping is not the same as that of two toes tapping, whereas, once upon a time, they were one and the same, according to Henrietta Armani.

3. Henrietta Armani wrrittes aa sttorry likke thhisss & callls ittt "EEEro" bbbutt therrre iis nnno "onccce uppponnn aaa tiiiime" inn hherr stttory, only little apple trees.

B. A Two-Sentence Story in Appreciation of the Cinematic.

1. Henrietta Armani lost herself in the movie, eating popcorn out of a box held between the knees of a

second person Henrietta Armani refused to call by name, this arising out of principles vaguely formulating in her head. She did not think of him as a pleasant companion.

C. A Three-Sentence Story, One of Them Foreign.

1. When Henrietta Armani arrived home from the movies some dark person seated in the darkened room Henrietta Armani was forced to pass through in order to find herself in her own room said to whoever it was the dark person in the darkened room he (or she) thought it was (or might be) he (or she) was saying this to, "Who goes there?"

¿Quién va ahi?

D. A Multi-Sentence Story in Which the Key Word Is "Door."

1. Henrietta Armani was intensely distressed and embarrassed that the room she entered possessed a doorway but the doorway possessed no door. It seemed to Henrietta Armani when she entered her doorless room that a darkness entered with her, which was darker than the darkness already in residence; in daylight this did not happen; i.e., the light did not brighten when she entered the doorless room – which failure, Henrietta Armani reasoned, must have something to do with the kind of person she was.

Yes. Henrietta Armani thought this even as she piled heavy boxes in the doorway, these boxes held together by baling wire which she now had no more of because the baling wire had vanished from her room while she had sat in the darkened movie theatre with an unnamed person.

Why did the house in which she now resided have no electricity? When she had rented the room a radio had been playing. She distinctly remembers. The room may or may not have had a door.

E. A Henrietta Armani Story Composed of Brief Declarative Sentences, with Footnotes.

1. Henrietta Armani, alone in her room, says, "I will."[1] She says, "I will not."[2] She says, "Why are you pestering me?"[3] She says, "I hate you."[4] She says, "I wish you would drop dead."[5] She says, "I am such a lunatic."[6] She says, "Don't tell me I can't, if I want to."[7] She says, "This carpet is filthy."[8] She says, "That is the strangest thing."[9] She says, "I am eating an apple."[10] She says, "I applied today for three jobs."[11] She says, "What went with my money?"[12] She says, "Do you have a parakeet?"[13] She says, "You are an everlasting pill."[14] She says, "I refuse to tell you where I live."[15] She says, "I did not like it either."[16] She says, "Tomorrow I will try again."[17] She says, "If you do not like it you know what you can do with yourself."[18] She says, "Don't you just wish that was so!"

The footnotes:

[1] "I bet you will change your mind."

[2] "You always do."

[3] "Why don't you calm down?"

[4] "Did I ever say I wanted to marry you?"

[5] "Be nice."

[6] "We all have troubles."

[7] "What does *that* mean?"

[8] "I suppose that's my fault also."

[9] "What? What is the strangest thing?

[10] "I distinctly heard you say, 'What is that noise?'"

[11] "You won't get them."

[12] "You are always flying off somewhere."

[13] "Don't be silly."

[14] "Ditto, sweetheart."

[15] "Who wants to know?"

[16] "The movie?"

[17] "The doorman will not let you in."

[18] "I could have the police lock you up.

F. Another Henrietta Armani Story Beginning with "When." The Saddest Story.

When Henrietta Armani went to the bar on Amsterdam Ave. she sat first at the bar and then in a booth, with no action at either. She sat at the bar again, and the barperson who of course was interested in her said, "You again." After saying pour me another of what I had the other times, Henrietta Armani said, "What is the saddest story you ever heard?" To which the barperson, a decent sort who had been deserted as a child, of course said, "My own."

"Tell it to me," Henrietta Armani said, and the barperson would have done, each night of his many nights behind the bar had been waiting to do so. But the pool players wanted coins for their tables. An officious person on another stool at the long bar wanted a scotch and soda. A beer keg was foaming over.

In the absence of the barperson's sad story Henrietta Armani told herself her own story, which was not the story her brain wanted to hear, although her body was content to have Henrietta Armani struggle through it. "It will have you in tears," Henrietta Armani said to no one.

"Everyone I know is dolefully waiting out the hours."

She did not know who said this.

Afterwards, the barperson appeared again, saying, "I do not like to see your head on the table."

"Which table?" asked Henrietta Armani. She was again in a booth, and did not know how she had got there. The barperson's voice was a nice voice which conveyed no malice.

Henrietta Armani said to this nice voice, "I do not wish you to think I am alcoholic," being quite amazed to discover that not a single person was paying her the smallest attention.

"What is this?" she asked, and when she turned her head to examine the one thing, which was on the table beside her two hands along with the other thing, the other thing of its own volition lifted up and dribbled its contents down her throat, which was both a magical and an exasperating experience.

"Since my divorce," Henrietta Armani said, "I trust no one. But I trust you."

The face she said this to, someone passing, said, "You should eat something."

She was sick for a great while and did not in the least mind.

G. A Continuation of Henrietta Armani's 'Saddest' Story

Henrietta Armani walked down a long hall covered with grit and through another door marked with the notice DO NOT ENTER – only to discover behind the forbidden door a deserted kitchen containing two stainless steel tables with numerous gleaming objects of a practical nature hanging above the tables.

That is what she saw once she saw them.

Before this sighting she had to determine which of the many switches on the wall on this side of the DO NOT ENTER door worked to illuminate such gleaming objects, since, until that moment, the room, her head and its body, had all been wrapped in total darkness.

She switched this one switch off and on for a good many minutes, out of purest pleasure, because her own ex-husband, Mr. Demented, had once hung perhaps this very sign outside the door he went through each day or evening, after saying to the still air, "I must go and compose myself."

This had transpired in a certain house, one vividly locked in her mind, which she believed had been located in the country. *Willow Run* were two words which seemed to her to sound familiar.

If she had on her person now a road map, she bet she could find it.

Each evening she had driven a car, the blue car, with her daughter strapped into the daughter's back safety seat, to meet the 6:15 train from the city. Where she had parked there had been a sign which said PICK UPS ONLY. Her daughter in the back safety seat would throw her toys and she would retrieve them and return the toys to her daughter to throw again. She could hear herself saying things like, "We must not spoil our supper," and "You must be a good girl." Sometimes, "We must be good girls." One thing she often had said, and sometimes still did say, was, "This weather, I don't know, it is so bucolic."

It would be nice, she thought, and a composing thing to do, to hang a sign around her own neck, to hang it as that one had hung around his doorknob or as that other one did, not hanging, but nailed to a stick in the grass. Inasmuch as this sign hanging around her neck would be a thing which people must pay attention to. The sign would say, HERE COMES HENRIETTA ARMANI.

Her mother had only been comfortable with strangers, which was another thing she told herself she must think about this evening before she gave up the ghost and took a taxi home, assuming a taxi would take her there.

In her purse was the address, but where was her purse?

For that matter, where were her shoes?

On one of the several gleaming counters was a bowl of soup, Chicken Godiva, which someone had left for her, the note beneath it saying, "For you, Bubble Head."

Henrietta Armani, far from being offended, drank from the bowl with relish, wishing she could bother herself to seek out bread or crackers, but finding herself altogether too famished.

With Chicken Godiva soup the chicken was supposed to ride about naked, but in this soup the chicken had its clothes on.

Whatever, it was a very tasty soup.

There was a phone on the wall, with a stickum tab saying, *Trudy, call Travis*, but she was not either of these people, only wishing she might be so that she might hear what one said to the other, and advise them on the more effective alternatives.

The father – was this in a film? – had said, "Go ye and do likewise." This to her mind did not sound like the sort of thing her father would say to her, or say to another father, although he possibly could more than once have said it to her mother.

Why were they not inquiring about her, by the way? They had not inquired about her in a long time, months, although they knew her number, although it was the wrong number.

The *wrong* number would be the number of the old house, the family house, *her* house, though it had always been the wrong number. The new house did not have a number any more than it had electricity or a door to her room other than stacked boxes.

Who had packed those boxes? She certainly had not dirtied her hands packing boxes. Packing them with what Mr. Degenerate said was to be *her* things, not *his* things, not their daughter's things, nor those things which were so ambiguous they seemed to her to be the things belonging to no one on this planet.

Which she had told him – words to that effect – their daughter crying, but he had said, "You are not making sense."

He had said, "Go and take something."

Which she thought had meant, "Put something in a box," which she had done, a picture from the wall along the staircase, to which he had said, "Why do you want that? Why in God's name do you think I am going to let you have a picture of my *grandmother?*"

To which she had said, "God in heaven, *that* is your grandmother? I thought that picture was *my* grand-mother!"

To which he had said, picking up and holding their crying daughter, "You are out of it, you know. By God, you are out of it today, you know!"

To which she had said – in a place called *Willow Run* she had said this – "Well, they were both *ministers*, you know!" Which made no sense to her now, although it had then, and it was certainly true that on both sides they had all been ministers of one kind or another, as proved by the little crosses each held up in the one hand, in whatever old sepia photograph existed of them.

"I'd advise you to go to bed."

Him saying that, and their daughter struggling to release herself from his arms, saying, "May I go too?" And then saying, or someone saying, *"Daddy, why are you hurting me?"*

H. More of the Henrietta Armani 'Saddest' Story.

In the bar, the lights off, Henrietta Armani looked for other light switches, and could not find them, although of course there had to be switches.

Her new room had switches but these were not switches that turned anything on. The first evening, that person in the other dark room watching her through the doorless door, breathing on her, a machine beside him (or her) that breathed for him (or her), she had clicked the switch off and on, saying "*Off,*" saying "*On,*" and everything happening, like there was power in her fingertips if only she would keep on exerting herself and not sink into the desuetude, where she customarily – since *when?* – had been sinking.

Her room in the new place had a loose board in the floor. She must remember, when she got home to the new room, to be wary of the loose board. Well, really, every *other* board was loose, but loose boards were better than having to walk in her naked feet over a carpet so filthy you could see the diseases in the fibres bumping heads with each other.

I. A One-Sentence Story Describing Henrietta Armani's War with Rug Diseases.

Wwwhiich offf yyoou bbad ttthings ddidd ttthis tto mmmeeee uunnder the little apple trees?

J. A Longer Henrietta Armani Story Filled with Action.

She poured herself "*a dring, a drinkie,*" the finest, and sat first at the bar, then in the booth, then again on her favourite stool, where once upon a time she had been dangling a leg, smoking, when a man with bigoted intentions had said to her, "You are such a honey.

You are such a sweetie. You are such a tomato, I am delirious."

Then the man had sang *"Set'm up, Joe,"* which he said was a song someone named "Frankie" had made famous during his, the man's, youth.

The man flirting with her had a big paunch which he called a beer belly and he left the change from his drinks on the counter, all those dollars, while she lacked the courage ever to be so blatant about the amount she meant spending.

The men and women passing on Amsterdam, a few now and then, night owls with slumping shoulders, their bodies sinking into their shoes, all looked to her like people she had known at one time. Which was why she was sitting at the bar and not in the booth, so she would know them.

It did not alarm her *in the slightest* that they did not know her. More than once she said to herself, I am the Queen of the Planet, and each time she voiced this thought she would wait in silence for someone to issue denials.

She had her own answer, *You may be, but you are no better than me*, but she was waiting for an answer better and more spiritual in nature than that.

Another reason Henrietta Armani was sitting on the stool and not in the booth was because of what was behind the bar, on a shelf beneath the cash register under a wet J-cloth. Under there was a pistol which she had already explored. She had explored its handgrip, its black, snubby barrel, and the little twig of metal which anyone in her right mind would know was the trigger.

The pistol weighed, she estimated, about the same as three full drinks. In the movie she had seen with the man she was now so furious at there had been a weapon called a forty-five. She did not think this weapon, which for a while she had slid back and forth along the bar, was that weapon which, when you write it, is written point45. That is neat, she thinks, because these are things that when you use them you point them at someone, or at your own self, in the extreme case. "Like," she said aloud, "such is more productive than a sling shot."

K. Henrietta Armani Thinks She Would Like to Feed the City. Not the End of the Story.

Once three men shook the bar's door knob. Henrietta Armani was asleep on the stool when this happened, and knew nothing of this. Otherwise, she would have let them in and might have enjoyed herself.

Around five in the morning, daylight breaking, she went into the kitchen, breaking open into a gigantic crock every egg that could be found in the cooler, both the brown eggs and the white – close to two hundred. She was going to stir up eggs – bacon, if she could find it – for everyone.

The front door, however, would not open. It would not open from the inside. To open these grilled doors, they had to be opened from the *other* side. Which really was, to her way of thinking, a pathetic situation. People, clearly, would want breakfast. Already, gauging by the assemblage, there was an interest.

Henrietta Armani decided she would stir up the eggs in any case, since, otherwise, life had no meaning.

Home fries, bacon, a sprinkle of – the red stuff. Yes, not anise, not chili, but the red stuff. Not coriander, not thyme, not oregano or curry powder, none of which were red.

It amused and embarrassed her that she could not think of the name of the red thing.

Henrietta Armani had been known as an exceptionally gifted chef at one point in her life.

Because she couldn't remember, she took the eggs off the grill and went and made herself three tall drinks, lining these up on the bar, better to do the weight test again with the pistol which was not a point45 that was to be pointed at someone.

Cayenne.

Naturally.

The right word came when you were not thinking about what the right word was.

Cayenne, of course, was not exactly red.

Whereas "Bastards" was a word which fell off the tongue like leaves from autumn trees.

Which was another song – *the autumn leaves of red and gold drift by my window* – that man with the beer belly claimed a person named "Frankie" had made his specialty.

She was not herself keenly interested in or much moved by romantic ballads, even in stereo wraparound at the movie house.

Dress the egg dish with clawed tomatoes, sprigs of parsley, why not watercress? She had done this all her life, bibs for the three of them because bibs seemed so attractively old-fashioned and certainly the baby required one.

"Oh, yes," she said, "you are right, I stand corrected, that was ages ago."

To grow your own watercress, if you have not a river or spring or pool of flowing water, prick sizable holes in your tub, fill this container with black earth, install and tamp your seeds, then bring your hose to the tub and leave your hose running for the balance of your years on earth, to thence awaken each day of every year, your tub overflowing with an abundance of the finest product.

Which was what she had done in her marriage, precisely as instructed.

"So sit yourself down and partake," she told herself, seated at the bar with a plate of rock-hard eggs, the pistol, and the two remaining tall drinks.

Which was how Henrietta Armani was found when at eleven a.m. another barperson opened the

Amsterdam Bar doors – another decent human being, whistling, tinkering with the heavy chains, then entering, thinking to himself as he saw her slumped there in the dead, shadowy air: "Why, there sits Mother!"

L. Mr. Bottle the Neighbour.

Mr. Bottle the neighbour built ships inside bottles, which ships each had the name, Mrs. Bottle.

Henrietta Armani was eight years old when Mr. Bottle invited her to forego her cartwheels on his lawn and experience the greater joy; to wit, to venture inside his lovely tract home and he would show her his bottles.

Mr. Bottle's bottles were all arrayed upon a white mantle, each sailing along splendidly inside the glass, although Henrietta Armani was more interested in Mr. Bottle's dress code.

She said, "Why is all that hair on your chest?"

To which Mr. Bottle responded by showing her his newest bottle, inside the bottle what he said was a ship known as a Shapper, invented by a Mr. Shapper, Esquire, of Birmingham, England, many many years ago, the special attribute of Mr. Shapper's ship being that it possessed virtually no leg room above deck, save that needed for wrapping sails and coiling ropes and something called the "Grig." While below deck, in that space Mr. Shapper called "the hole," in agreement with other ship designers, there was immense space for the oars, the oarsmen, the slaves, plus a chapel where a good man would preach the Africans conversion.

Mr. Bottle told her all this and more, apparently having the highest opinion of Mr. Shapper's attributes.

"My dear, you see here all my ships are named the same name, Mrs. Bottle, not even employing numbers, as you see, because all women are exactly the same, they are all Mrs. Bottle insofar as Mr. Bottle is concerned, which I recognize as a gross exaggeration although it still seems to me to be the straight-out gospel truth, the Christian truth, although I will ask you to leave now, my darling, because you are such a nice girl, so lovely doing your cartwheels, before I or Mrs. Bottle decide that we must hurt you."

The truth being, as Henrietta Armani decided later, that Mr. Bottle, while deluded, was the first gentleman of her encounter, and far more advanced in the decorum of his thinking than any of those others with whom she afterwards had a relationship. Most of all inclusive in this her relationship with the man who said "I do" to her face, and kissed her, and from that moment turned inconceivably evil.

You do not have to go through with this was a phrase which all her waking days post-marriage existed as a plague in the mind of Henrietta Armani.

She had not shown *pluck* in removing herself from the worshipful courtship of the man suing for her affection.

M. Husbandry: A 'Sadder' Page in Henrietta Armani's 'Saddest' Story.

Give me your poor and your disabled, he had said.

This, on their honeymoon. He had been quoting, imprecisely, the script on the plaque in New York City harbour. Henrietta Armani had believed he was addressing, personally, certain shores of herself that had not yet surfaced.

She had thought his words addressed her essence, which essence his quotation was meant to sincerely applaud, and thus she could now share her secrets with him, as soon she would share her body – provided *she went through with it* – and Henrietta Armani had welcomed the degenerate into to her bosom – into her arms, spectacularly.

Not that this, her body, had seemed to make an impression on him.

N. Henrietta Armani's Daughter, a Child Prodigy.

Her daughter, in conversation with grownups, would say, "I am not a conversationalist."

To illustrate the point, she would then spill something on something precious.

There were hack marks on the furniture, which wounds in the fine wood pointed the way to future serious problems. Had Henrietta Armani been psychologically or psychically attuned to take notice.

Not that she *didn't*, of course.

The question was what to do about it, other than to have a seasoned restorer of fine wood come in and restore the fine wood.

Or drape their surfaces with cloth.

Both of these measures, as a matter of fact, were measures taken.

When Henrietta Armani first saw the child carving holes in the furniture, gouging the blade of her knife into the polished wood, the child had both heard and seen her, *looked* at her, but had gone on with her ruinous work on the elegant furniture.

Much later, several years, even though Henrietta Armani saw their dog being run over by a perfect stranger, when she saw the dead dog either actually or in her mind, she had been overcome with suspicions.

She said to her husband, "We have a disturbed child."

In answer to this he had settled his tableware all but silently over his Beef Wellington, crossed to her chair at the opposite table end, and struck her.

Her daughter said, "Why can't I chase cars too? Who is to stop me?"

O. Other Ingredients in the 'Saddest' Part of Henrietta Armani's 'Saddest' Story.

"If you want to speak to me," the child would say to her father, "why not speak to me? I like listening."

The trouble with Henry – how odd it was, Henrietta Armani often thought – to actually say his name – is that when he stopped to think, he stopped entirely.

The trouble with her, with Henrietta Armani, is that when she stopped, the last thing she wanted to do was think.

When she stopped she wanted *it* to be over. Therefore, often – wherever she was and with who and whomever it was she was doing whatever she was doing, Henrietta Armani stopped abruptly. She stopped what she was doing.

The man she went to for help, who had been her friend and who loved eating buttered popcorn in the movies, would say, when she stopped, "What are you doing?"

They would have their clothes off, at his place or at her place or at the place of a third party, and he would say that. The air would be cold on her skin because of the sweat. Her flesh would be pebbly.

She would not look at him at such times, because of how he was looking.

At the movie, the popcorn between his legs, she had sometimes, to be playful, allowed her fingers to clutch like claws where the popcorn wasn't.

He had made it clear to her that he did not find this amusing. Yet he also was not amusing, because often when she got home she would find butter stains on her skirt where he had wiped his hands. Which was not a friendly thing for him to have done, which was not a thing he would have done had he not believed, as he frequently was saying, that she was eating more than her share of the popcorn.

So there were these times but also those other times when he did not like it at all that she had suddenly stopped what it was she had been doing. He would glower at her, and say hurtful things, if she stopped. So Henrietta Armani stopped stopping. She also stopped seeing him at all, with precisely that same abruptness. She did agree to this much. "I will see you outdoors. I will see in such places where we can be publicly seen, seated."

He said, "Why should I want to see you publicly? Why should I be interested."

Which provided her with a revelation as to his character, which she found interesting.

"But I thought you went to him for help," another friend said. Which was such a silly thing to say that she stopped seeing this other friend, who in a score of ways had proved herself to be a False Friend.

When Henrietta Armani passed this False Friend on the street she was inclined to say, initially, "Hello, False Friend." Later on, she learned to keep her tongue silent. Banter, insults, the tight expressions, she was finding disagreeable.

She would try secretly to wave at the small child the False Friend carried, to be sure. A child, her own included, was an innocent party. It hurt her to hurt innocent parties, such as her own child who was as innocent as any, despite the ferocity with which her child remarked on things.

Such as, "Why did you smile at that stupid baby?"

Over a long period afterwards, when one of these False Friends called – there were so many – and her innocent daughter lured her to the phone, the phone she held in her one hand as she listening to a familiar voice on the phone saying, "What are you doing," she passed the phone over to her other hand – to the hand that was doing nothing until that moment – both she and her daughter then looking at the one hand that was now the new empty hand doing nothing except twist the cord, as if both she and her daughter were thinking that surely that empty hand – something – must have the answer.

Eventually these people stopped calling.

The pain of those days so amazed Henrietta Armani that when she looked back on them afterwards it was as though her skin was crawling with venomous lizards.

Her husband said, "That sounds like a bad dream. Please know that I find all dreams boring."

P. Henrietta Armani's Wide Scholarship as This Relates to Her 'Saddest' Story.

Henrietta Armani read in a magazine that the answer resides in the heavens. In the molecules, the dust, of ancients who are in sojourn on their endless journey. A journey into nothingness, which goes on forever. There they are, she can sometimes see them, see their faces, their mouths opening, but these ancients have no answer either. They speak platitudes. "There, there, my girl, it will be over soon." Because time for them has now become nothingness. Two o'clock, ten o'clock, the day, the month, the year, means zip to them. They say to her, these ancients do, "You are making too much of something that is essentially trivial." By which they mean her life. Where they have arrived at, disembodied except when they speak, all existence, including their own, is without meaning. They are lucky because they no longer have to search for it.

If particles of dust contain the souls of her ancestors – where's the joy in that?

They are people in strange form, in strange solitudinous journey, but otherwise they are as lost as she is.

St. Paul in her dreams says to his brethren, "Put to the test, all of you would say you abhor women."

St. Paul – on both sides of what had constituted her family – was a gentleman that family had been fond of quoting.

One evening she said to her husband, "Excuse me, but to my mind your St. Paul was something of a bastard."

She had thought he would rise from the table and strike her. What he had done instead was to say to their daughter, seated between them, "Release your fork. Put down your napkin. Rise from your chair. Now go to your mother and slap her hard as you can."

When Henrietta Armani painted her lips during those days, she painted them outside the borders of her lips' natural formation. She did this out of nasty intention. When she spoke, if she decided she would, she wanted people who knew no more about the issues than she did to listen to her.

Similarly, her eyes.

Sometimes her daughter would say, "Why isn't Henrietta wearing her pearls?"

At times we were shockingly close is Henrietta Armani's view.

Q. The Inspirational in the Unhappy Life of Henrietta Armani.

What Henrietta Armani most sought from life was the inspirational. It delighted her, its common occurrence. Always, even at her lowest ebbing, she saw things that were utterly amazing. Which is to say, inspirational. Sunsets did amaze her, although sunsets were not so much as even in the realm of what it was she was talking about when she talked to her daughter about life's abundant marvels.

On evenings not that long ago from the back door, Henrietta Armani saw gypsy wagons on a road. She saw this where no road existed. The gypsies were so robustly singing that her daughter, upstairs in her room, shouted down, "Who is that singing?"

Henrietta Armani, one day, saw from her kitchen window a wild boar. The boar was leading one of its young up to her back door. She opened the door and the boars ate all that she dropped to the floor. Then the boars returned to the forest, where there was no forest. Her daughter, entering, had said, "What did you feed them?"

Henrietta Armani had only to open the door, to stand by a window, and the inspiring would find her.

It was not required that the inspirational be spectacular.

Hippos immersed themselves in muddy streams by the side of the house.

On a fine Sunday, Charlie Chaplin in hobo attire knocked at her door. She invited Charlie inside. She made Charlie a nice breakfast. Charlie sang and danced for her. He said to her, "Venture down the road with me. This little trick I do with my big shoes, my cane, my hat, I will teach you. Come. You will find the method useful."

R. The End of the Henrietta Armani Story

Ended, bang, just like that.

The bartender entered, saw the form draped over the bar. An indrawn breath as he said in full surprise, "Why, there sits mother!"

Henrietta Armani had not got far in composing what was to have been her final message.

On the floor he discovered Henrietta Armani's purse. Inside the purse a message and telephone number scribbled on an empty envelope: Here comes Henrietta Armani, Call this Number.

Over the coming days he would try this number, the telephone always ringing, no one answering.

He devised innumerable alternatives, none rewarded.

Kelly Watt

THE THINGS MY DEAD MOTHER SAYS

I'm not sure if I'm going mad in Mexico or having a revelation about death. My mother and I didn't talk for five years. But now that she's dead we talk every day. I sat outside in the sun this morning, having awakened late, and she said: "This is where I sat and had my coffee every morning. Right where you're sitting now. Isn't it beautiful? Now you know why I came here."

The mid-day sun was heating up the octagonal tiles. They were bleached from so much Mexican mopping. Two wasps fornicated mid-air then hit the ground. Bougainvillea grew in red clusters up the wall. I noticed then that the door had an iron arch. I thought of my mother sitting there every morning with her coffee alone, following that arc, wondering about the meaning of life.

"Weren't you sad here, weren't you lonely?" I asked her.

"No, I always liked living alone."

She lived alone in so many one-bedroom apartments like this. It's odd. This one is exotic with its colonial stone walls, its *boveda* ceiling and yellow tile, but they all seem like the same apartment to me now. They all remind me of that first one – the basement apartment from my childhood on Kingston Road in Toronto with its subterranean air and intrepid noises from next door: a cat meowing; the opening of a closet door; the hammering of nails against a shared wall.

This morning in San Miguel de Allende there was a surprising sound – a baby squawking. Surprising because it's mostly old women who live in the complex now. *Casa Muerte*, a neighbour joked. They are all far away from their families and countries of origin. They have come here to eke out the last of their days in comfort and sunshine or solitude. But it's one thing to retire in Mexico, another thing to die here.

Lying on my mother's luxurious king mattress after the hospital bed had been removed, I realized I could see straight out the door, through the living room. The back of the sofa was visible and part of the front door. I was reminded of a Feng Shui rule. It was said that if your bed was directly opposite the door, you would leave the room feet first. Exactly how my mother had left.

Her feet. Simple girl's toes rimmed with old nail polish. That startled me at first. The left over polish looked like blood. Her skin had gone alabaster by then, white as the stone sculpture beside the bed of the Venus without arms, without a head. My mother had only one working arm by then. The other had been taken by some furtive explosion in her brain, the hand curling in toward her groin, as if protecting herself from violation. Her mind went too after several days, her staring unnerving us all. I called the *farmacia* when she stopped blinking. *La doctora* came and bent over my mother with her stethoscope, calling my mother's name: "Barbara, Barbara." The accent on the wrong syllable. My mother's mouth lay open, her breath raspy and desperate, her eyes rolling up into the whites, but she didn't respond.

"How was it, Mom?" I asked her afterwards. Death, I meant.

"It hurts," she said.

La doctora was a charming pixie with short brown hair and little green crocs, dimpled cheeks. She had lifted her ear from the stethoscope and said: "I think she has had a stroke. I'm so sorry. She cannot talk to us anymore now."

"She cannot talk to us anymore," I repeated in shock. She cannot talk.

Later, I climbed up to the terrace, to scan the stars for hopeful signs. The Mexican new moon wore a wicked grin. In her studio, I found my mother's last painting. She had drawn a headless body outlined in green. Surrounded by darkness. The right side was

49

gone. The left hand curled inwards. There were no calves, no feet, a woman suspended as if in a bed. A premonition? I would never be able to ask her when she painted it because she could not talk to us anymore.

The hospice workers arrived soon after. The palliative care nurse was Guadalupe. Large, big-bellied Guadalupe with the impassive Indian face and long straight hair, a gentle measured voice, a way of talking as though shushing a crying child.

"It is for the best," she soothed me. "Your mother, she is not coming back now. She has had a stroke and the breathing will be getting shallower and shallower until it stops. Now we have to move to a new level of the hospice care for she won't suffer. I will outline the options to you now…"

My tears fell like raindrops on the wooden table. What had my mother said to me before she went? What had I said? What had we not said? That was worst of all.

I love you.

This is the end.

Why were we so stubborn?

I chose the most expensive and painless option.

"Good," Guadalupe said, "because otherwise the cancer is spreading now into her brain and lungs. She will be suffocating to death. It's not to scare you, but so that you know and can base your decision on the facts."

The facts. I sat on my mother's massive Aztec bed, staring at the faces carved into the posts, while they hooked her up to the intravenous. My beautiful mother. My fearless feisty mother who had dressed up as Bonnie in *Bonnie and Clyde* and marched around with a cigarette in one hand and a toy machine gun in the other. My mother who had leapt into a fountain at a fancy-dress ball when she grew bored of the dreary doctors' speeches. My mother who had sashayed down runways modelling fur coats at sixteen years old. My glorious invincible mother who had married a jazz drummer, a famous anaesthetist, and a pedophile, not in that order. Her mouth was now open, her breath rasping, her eyes staring. I was instructed to wet little cotton pads and put them over her eyes to keep them moist and closed.

"She will not be able to talk but she will be hearing you, so you can talk to her," Guadalupe went on. "Tell her you love her and are taking care of her. Speak to her in a calm voice. Do not cry. This is for the best. She is going to go with God now and will not be in pain much longer."

The assistant nurse, Maria, combed my mother's grey-blond hair into a topknot. Guadalupe and Maria put pillows under both of her arms so that she looked like a queen, holding court, wearing cream puff sunglasses, her teeth showing, her breath growing more gentle, more relaxed as the chemical peace in the I.V. did its work.

I held her feet. Her delicate feet that would lead the way eventually out the door, marvelling at how beautiful they were. Swollen but flawless. How flawless was the body in the end anyway? How intricate and efficient. How could all that symmetry be so suddenly usurped?

I massaged her feet with cream. The little toes surrendering. Each one so distinct. The third toe curling inward shyly. When the nurses left I massaged her hands. The rings were gone. The maid had stolen them. Along with the credit cards, her FM3, her wallet and her last will and testament. The friend had accused the maid, while the maid had accused the friend. All in Spanish. They had shouted at one another outside my mother's room while she lay dying, until I realized they were both guilty, kicked them out and changed the locks on the door.

Still, I could see the tan lines from where the rings had been. Only two weeks ago she had been walking and talking. Now she was this alabaster half-woman wrapped in a yellow sheet, smelling of shampoo and rotting apples.

I did as Guadalupe instructed, spoke to her gently as I went about my errands. On the last day, I returned to find her resting between breaths. I knelt over my mother's bed and whispered into her ear. I told her I loved her and would take care of everything. I told her she could go when she'd had enough. I would take care of her little dog and her crazy friend. She didn't move or make a sound, but she went right after. Quietly.

I sat, cross-legged, repeating a Buddhist prayer a teacher had taught me long ago: *May she be free of suffering, may she be at peace*. Waiting. Floating on the great white boat of the bed. Watching the leaping flames of the beeswax candles, their shadows conquering the ceiling. Inhaling the fragrant breath of the pink lilies. The fountain burbling along with the oxygen machine. Someone turned the oxygen machine off in the other room and there was a woosh then, a protracted sigh that exploded in my mind into a movie reel of our life together. As if it was I who was dying.

My glamourous Lana Turner mother appeared coming to pick me up on the bus, a vision in a pillbox hat. I watched her packing the polka-dot valise with all my things to send me off to the home for little girls every week. The little plates with the egg yolks dried onto them piled in the sink on weekends. Friday nights we cuddled in front of the TV. The sound of a plane overhead out in the backyard of our basement apartment, everything it said and didn't say about our loneliness and fragility in our world without men. The unfortunate wedding after a snowstorm on Valentine's Day. Walking among the snowdrifts on the way to the car, I sang the funeral march instead of the wedding march until my mother told me to shut up. The nasty divorce and subsequent dark years in the windowless apartment that shook whenever the streetcars went by. The happy wedding in the backyard to the anaesthetist. The Spastic Band that played on the patio, the dining-room table invisible for all the roast beef and salmon. Her sleek Jaguar with its new leather smell.

In those days, there was a box of Chardonnay in the study that was never empty. Our wet evenings began so optimistically. We had a screaming match outside the windy restaurant by the lake after I'd told her the truth.

"You left me, you left me there, they hurt me at the home for little girls. Then you married that creep!" I accused her.

"I never left you," she said. "They never hurt you. You must be imagining things."

After she divorced the anaesthetist and ran away to Florida we spent New Year's Eve at her apartment in Naples. We wore silly party hats and did Gypsy cards to foretell our futures. Hoping for new love and dolphins. New love never came. We sat on the beach for hours waiting for the dolphins to appear, but they didn't come either that season. In Guatemala, we took turns puking that last night in the hotel. Lying awake at dawn, laughing at our predicament in twin beds. The older Mexican women on the trip often said: "You must take care of your mother." But she was so difficult to take care of, so angry. Nothing I did made her happy by then.

All the years she was angry at me, followed by all the years I was angry *igualmente*… They flashed by in an instant, rendered suddenly unimportant by death. All the words forgotten, all the misunderstandings erased. Underneath it all was only our strange shared journey where we had sometimes held hands, and sometimes not, in various Latin-American locations. All of it leading to this moment, where she would die in San Miguel de Allende.

Once she was gone I feared a vengeful ghost. What if the angry blaming mother appeared? But that's not what happened. She emerged youthful, unblemished and intact, smiling, happy to be free. My lovely young mother. The version I had liked the most.

"It's going to be okay, Sam," she said, and stroked my head the way I had been stroking hers these last days. I sat on her bed and cried. For in the end, what was there but love? Love present or love denied, it was always the same in the end. Once she was gone I wanted her back, but she told me: "That was it, kiddo, that was all the time we had."

They were far too quick with the removal of the body. I watched helpless as they wrapped the sheet around her face and plunked her onto a gurney. They wanted passport photos and forms signed. Suddenly I couldn't remember my grandmother's maiden name.

There were too many strangers in the room. The man at the door was smiling, "*Buenas noches,*" as if delivering pizza. "*¿Cómo está?*"

How the fuck do you think I am? I wanted to shriek, but I said *Buenas noches,* feeling myself slipping into absurdity.

Guadalupe and the funeral driver chatted and filled out paperwork in the living room, while I slipped out into the courtyard. It was dark, the wind was blowing, dried pink bougainvillea leaves scuttled about, making hollow scraping noises. The winds of time, the winds of change, I thought. Nothing will ever be the same. My hair blew into my eyes and I was temporarily blind. I wanted to scream, you can't take her yet, but I couldn't talk any longer. I stood by the black hearse. There was no glass in the back window. Just like the restaurants in Mexico. Everything open to the air. There was only a small canvas curtain. I could see my mother's still body inside. I didn't want anyone else to touch her. I wasn't sure I should trust her to this windowless car, to these men who spoke no English. I reached in my hand and cradled her head. Her hair was so thin I could feel her skull, fragile, small under my touch. The skull of a child. Or a young girl. Perfectly shaped. Still. Not yet cold.

I wanted to keep my hand there forever. I stood there holding her head, crying fat tears onto the cobblestones at my feet. Then they drove her away.

That night I lay staring at the ceiling, still feeling my mother's skull in my palm. My thoughts looping. I thought of how sometimes Buddhas were depicted holding a skullcap. What is a skullcap? I'd often wanted to know. But of course now I understood – it was the shaman's ultimate instrument, the human skull, the top of the head. In *tangkas,* Tibetan religious paintings done on silk, it was often depicted filled with precious jewels. Why was it filled with jewels? I wondered. *Because death is the jewel,* I heard in my head. I had touched my mother's skullcap and known death. It was so simple it was shocking. I now knew the truth: death could come so suddenly. Without premonition. It was always with us, dancing like the grim reaper at the Indian parades in the *jardine* in San Miguel.

The next morning there was too much wailing to hear her voice. The day after that I had to drive to the crematorium and choose a receptacle. I chose the plain black box. Homage to *2001: A Space Odyssey.* It seemed appropriate for the central mystery that was unfolding. I brought my mother home soon after in her new abode. It seemed impossible that my mother's white feet, her perfect toes, her long body and mystical skullcap were now reduced to ashes in a small black box, a piece of paper with a date and stamp on it.

I put the black box on a table with her favourite Casablanca lilies. Taped a photo onto the box of her smiling, wearing a blue sweater. A photo from better times, happier times. I bought white candles wrapped in paper stamped with blue nuns. But the candles kept falling over. They were wobbly nuns. Finally I had to prop them up in plastic cups. The stamped paper caught fire as the candles burned down. The plastic melted and there was spilt wax all over the altar. When I went to clean the glass, I lifted up the black box and heard the rushing of sand inside, a knocking of bone against wood.

The first words I heard her say were: "I fucked up, Sam, I fucked up."

She meant that she hadn't realized she was so ill, so she hadn't gone to the doctor, she had neglected her own health.

But I calmed her: "No, Mom you didn't fuck up, you just didn't know. It was a sneaky cancer, asbestos, it crept up on you, a stealthy foe with guerilla tactics while you stood facing the open field waiting for the enemy to present itself."

"I'm sorry," she said. Apologizing for the past, the home for little girls, the husband who violated little children. Then she said, "He isn't here," meaning my beloved stepfather. I was worried she was lost then in some in-between world, trapped in psychic purgatory, unable to stay or go.

One week later, I borrowed books on death from the Shambhala Centre. *The Tibetan Book of the Dead* states that one mustn't cry or the dead find it hard to leave. But wouldn't they be insulted too if no one shed a tear? I lay on her bed and sobbed one entire afternoon. She came again then and brushed the hair off my face as she had when I was a girl, when we loved each other unequivocally. I felt her warm hand, I heard her voice as she said, "There, there, it's going to be okay. I'm okay," she said, and smiled. "Look at me!"

She cat-walked up and down the tile in the bedroom in front of me, changing form, showing off. Making me laugh. Becoming her twenty-year-old lithe self, all beehive and luminous eyes. Then her rounded cheerful thirty-year-old self with the platinum flip. She looked back at me, cheeky now in her well-preserved highlighted forties.

"I can't decide which to be," she said, as if choosing something to wear. "I can go anywhere, be anything."

I laughed and wondered if I was cracking up.

She was happy to be relieved of her body, of the house of her suffering. Happy to be in between.

I took to reading poems from *The Tibetan Book of the Dead* at night by candlelight, around the time of her death, 10:10 p.m. Lighting all the wobbly nuns I'd corralled into a planter.

When through strong unconscious tendencies I wander
*   in samsara,*
on the luminous light-path of innate wisdom,
may the vidyadhara warriors go before me
their consorts the host of dakinis behind me;

help me to cross the bardo's dangerous pathway
and bring me to the perfect Buddha state.

Reciting nightly, the dutiful daughter in death.

"You can stop reading the prayers now," she said one night. "I don't really like them. I don't know what they mean."

Oh, there was nothing written in the book about that.

While I planned her memorial she appeared again.

"Just remember the good things, Sam," she said. I had for a while, buoyed by the peacefulness of her death, she had not suffered long. I had come all this way to see to it. Had got on my knees in front of *La Virgen de Guadalupe* in the gothic cathedral and prayed: *Do not let her die in pain. Do not let her suffer. Let there be love and reconciliation between us.*

And there had been.

Still, I woke up sweating one morning, tormented by all the things I might have done differently. Maybe the faith healers who had appeared mysteriously at the door could have saved her after all, if only I'd called them back and paid all those pesos.

"No, Sam," she said, "it's all over. Let it go." My mother growing sage as God the closer she got to the light. Was that it? Or was it just my own voice in my head? Yet I could hear her. When I complained to her one night about how lonely I was, the next day, her friend appeared with my mother's little dog, Chelsea. A tiny schnauzer with enormous rabbit ears. She scampered through the house looking for my mother everywhere, sniffing through the clothes puddled in heaps on the floor. I was wearing my mother's velvet shirt. She stuffed her black nose into my armpit, wagged her tail then crawled into my lap.

She follows me from room to room now. her nose brushing up against my calves lest I disappear. I tried to discipline her to sleep in her dog bed on the floor, but one night she leapt onto the bed, then snuffled her way under the covers to lie beside me, her back to my back.

She puked on the carpet two days in a row. Kibble puke that I nearly stepped into, that smelled of roast chicken and baby poo. The mess stained my mother's wool carpet. I didn't know what to feed her.

"Feed her the smaller kibble," my mother shouted at me in the kitchen one afternoon. "Puppy kibble. It's in the plastic container in the pantry."

I went looking and found it. Go figure.

"Why are you shouting at me?" I said silently.

"Because I keep trying to tell you and you're not listening."

The dead must be hoarse from trying to get our attention.

November came. Over night the streets outside were full of altars for the Day of the Dead. *Ofrendas* in black and orange. Marigolds everywhere forming bold crosses. Candles in elaborate holders. I walked Chelsea to the Plaza Civica and discovered whole families on their knees creating mandalas for the dead, symbolic circles made out of beans, marigolds, and red bushy flowers with long stems. A photograph of the departed loved one in a frame at the head. An enormous speaker was erected in the courtyard playing dance music. The geometric mandalas were arranged around the fountain, fanning outwards like bright flags of grief and celebration. I circumambulated the fountain in awe of all these love letters to those who had passed. But when I went back the next morning they were gone. Erased. Only a few chalk smudges left on the pavement. I was chilled. How quickly we are here and gone. The whole event seemed like a crazed hallucination.

The next night I went to a gallery opening in honour of *Dia de los Muertos*. A butler dressed in skeleton makeup greeted everyone at the door. There were roving musicians. Special sugared bread and dried mango on a platter. The gallery was overflowing with the grey haired and distinguished. They strolled in their finery. Women sporting expensively coiffed hair and too many facelifts, the old who would not grow old. I took photographs of a papier-maché Katrina, a skeleton character with a wide-brimmed hat in fancy dress.

"Katrina means hope," the artist told me. "*Esperanza*. Hope never dies," he said.

I went to the bilingual bereavement group.

"Love hurts," the counsellor told me. Although she seemed to scold when she talked.

But does it need to hurt so much and so relentlessly? I wondered.

"I'm not ready to let go of her things," I said. "Her apartment."

"Is it because you want some of those things or because you are not ready to let go?"

"Both," I said, wondering why she found this difficult to understand. She had a degree in thanatology but the empathy of a lizard.

"You have to let go. You will have to go back, no? Will you not?"

"Yes," I said, "I hope one day I can come back to San Miguel de Allende."

"No, I mean, you will have to go back home to your own country."

"I'm not ready," I told her, "because when I give everything away, when I close up the apartment and lock the door it will be the end. There will be no more of my mother, of the woman I never really had enough of."

"But this is your work," she said, matter-of-factly, her green eyes fierce. "Eventually we have to say *adios*, no?"

Adios. Goodbye. It sounded so much more final in Spanish.

How could we not have talked to one another? How could we have wasted a moment of this brief dream of life to disagree? It seemed impossible now.

"Wherever you go your mother will be with you," my husband said. But he had never left his home-town. He reminded me Mexico was a dangerous place.

"A group of bandits hijacked a bus and left the tourists naked in the jungle," he told me.

"But that happened miles from here," I said. "And no one died."

"What's it like, death?" I ask my mother while packing up her photos.

"It's not what you think," she says, unwilling to give away the secret. "Go home to your husband," she says. "Don't stay here," she warns. "Your girlfriends won't take care of you the way he does."

Still bossy even in the afterlife.

I have sad days, then angry days.

"Why didn't you call me, Mom?" I chide her. "Why didn't you return my calls? Let me help you."

"I thought you didn't like me," she says.

"I was angry but that doesn't mean I didn't love you," I tell her.

"I know. I love you too, dear," she says.

I know then that she will look out for me.

I wallow in guilt for a few days. Then one night the key gets stuck in the lock. I am late for a reception. I struggle and swear, but it won't budge. While I stand fuming in the courtyard, a couple come along. They recognize me and introduce themselves. They were married in my mother's backyard. They are visiting for only twenty-four hours and invite me to lunch. If I had not been stuck in the courtyard I would never have met them. Still, the lock has to be replaced. The next day we sit and talk on their lumpy sofas.

"Lung cancer is usually a secondary cancer," she tells me. "Often brain cancer is first. She wasn't walking properly. We think she'd had a mini stroke, your mother, and wasn't herself for many years. We all tried to get her to go to a doctor. To get her to seek help. She wouldn't go. There is nothing you could have done to make anything turn out any different than the way it did."

I cry for hours, wake up strangely grateful, convinced my mother was behind this.

Still, I delay buying my return flight. I put things in boxes then take them back out: her horse puppet, her Mayan shaman, her fairy garden mask. I rearrange the paintings. Secretly I think if I stay here walking these tile floors I will always hear her voice saying: *You're going to be okay, Sam.* Telling me she loves me, telling me what to do, instructing me on the right kind of kibble to buy for the dog.

Darlene Madott

WAITING
(AN ALMOST
LOVE STORY)

*When thou dost ask me blessing, I'll kneel down
And ask of thee forgiveness:*
—William Shakespeare, *KING LEAR, V, iii, 10*

*And grief still feels like fear. Perhaps, more strictly,
like suspense. Or like waiting; just hanging about waiting for something to happen. It gives life a permanently
provisional feeling.*

—C.S. Lewis, *A GRIEF OBSERVED*

They undressed in the dark, so he did not see her hands
trembling. She said she had never made love to a man
she didn't know. He said, probably not to one you
knew, either. She imagined he laughed with his chin
tucked into his chest – a shy laugh, or very guarded. At
least he is intelligent, she thought. That made her feel

less ashamed. She tried talking to herself. It was either now or never, the feeling in her stomach a kind of drowning.

"I don't want to get pregnant."

"Do you think I *want* to make you pregnant?"

She lay under him in a kind of panic, tried to deaden all feeling, to concentrate on something else, but the panic caught up with her. He withdrew without coming. She was almost grateful. Was he a kind man? Maybe. Maybe not. She asked if he was angry. He drew his hand down across his eyes and lower face, like a man after he shaves.

"It never is good the first time," he said. "Our bodies need more time to get acquainted."

Franny thought, I will not give you time. I will not let you touch me.

When he called the next morning, there was the fresh smell of cut sweet grass blowing through the open window. She told him she thought she was pregnant; she had been with her husband just the once before she'd left and they had made love. She said this to frighten him off, so that he would not trouble her again. Her lie drew him closer. He offered to help. It was not his problem, she said. He asked if she still loved her husband, if it would force her back to him if her fears turned out to be real?

But was any of it real? She remembered waking in the night to the panic of railcars being uncoupled and coupled. The train going nowhere. Waiting. Summer had turned into a kind of waiting. A waiting to return. A waiting to bleed. For she really did not get her period. Something had dried up in her.

They started off in the morning with breakfast at a restaurant overlooking the sea. Then he took her to the Aquarium, where she saw for the first time beautiful coloured creatures that blossomed before her eyes like underwater fireworks. He told her their name – anemone – his eyes watching her lips as she repeated it. He never looked into her eyes.

Then he took her for a drive along the North Shore. He did not speak, and Franny lay back in the seat.

She had never known a more silent man. His silence angered her. She thought it wilful, like the silence her husband had used to punish her. She resolved not to care. But she felt hostile. So she hit him with questions. What did he want from life? Who was he? What work did he do? What did he have to say for himself?

He said nothing. And then nothing. He was resolute about this silence of his. She felt flush with anger. She told him that his silence was like that of a peasant – without expectation. He looked at her in surprise, as if he were about to say something, but she saw him change his mind. So she lay back in the seat, resolved to forget about him. With the windows fully open and the air so warm, she dozed. They stopped twice. Once, to take a short walk into the rain forest, and then to explore a small fishing village where he bought her ice cream. By the time they arrived back in the evening, her face was burnt from the sun and sea air.

Hours after she had asked her questions and forgotten them, he told her his ambition had been to own one of those homes they had seen along the North Shore, to be a millionaire by thirty. He hadn't a doubt he could have done it. He told her that when he was a teenager he had bought a rowboat with a small motor, and had used to spend his Sundays gazing up at the cliffs, at the homes that looked, not down at him bobbing in the sea, but out at nothing, their windows as if blinded. A false dream. Like most desire, he said. He knew better at thirty. She wondered what had happened in his life to make him so devoid of expectation?

He ordered something not on the menu, something she had never tasted before – silken tofu in lotus leaf, with sliced shallot and enoki mushrooms. As each dish came to their table, he served the food onto her plate, as if to make sure that she was eating enough, as if this were a long habit of his, to fill the plates of the people with whom he ate. She was charmed. The tofu tasted like air, like she was feeding on air. She touched his ankle with her sandalled foot. She told him she had not felt any hunger for days. He had given her back her appetite. He grasped her foot between his two and held it there.

Above the table, he never took her hand, hardly spoke. He looked always down, always away from her. She thought, he is not an easy man. He does not seem to need anything.

"Look at me," she said.

He would not look at her. She was sure his eyes were a pale blue, almost colourless. He reached down and put his warm hand around her foot, between the instep and the sandal. Then he gave the foot a tug, so that, like a bobbin on water, her body dipped down at the tug. She clutched the table for support and laughed like a schoolgirl at how silly that must have looked. His strange affection pleased her.

"I know nothing about you."

"What do you need to know?"

"Who you are, what you do."

He said, "You can't judge a man by what he does for a living."

She thought, then: it must be something that embarrasses him.

"You've told me nothing about your past."

He said he wanted to stop at a bakery before taking her home. He was going to buy her cakes for her breakfast the next morning. He had noticed she was too thin.

He risked a glance in her direction and chuckled. She saw that she was right about his laugh, that he laughed inwardly with his chin tucked into his chest. She saw the pain she could cause with her questions.

"Why aren't you married?"

"I don't need a wife. I can do everything for myself." The directness of his answer made her laugh.

Was that all a wife meant?

Or was he giving her fair warning? Wasn't he saying they might be lovers, but he was not going to marry her?

At that she really laughed. Not to worry, she said. She had no *designs* upon him. In any case, she would be gone in a few months.

Franny let herself out of the car. She slammed the door. She did not take his box of pastries.

One day they met where the trolleys loop in Stanley Park and made the seven-mile walk around the seawall together. They had not brought their bathing suits or towels. At Second Beach, she lay back in the sand, overcome by the heat, and he half-sat, half-lay beside her, his hand under her head so that her long hair would not fill with sand.

He told her she was not pregnant. She did not have the look of a pregnant woman. Her body was just upset. It could be anything, he said – the journey out.

He touched her stomach through her sundress and told her to stop worrying, there was nothing *in* there.

The dress she was wearing was a pale blue cotton with thin shoulder straps. It had a full skirt, and she loved the freedom of walking in it, loved the way the wind would catch it and wrap it around her legs. It was an old dress. She had bought it for her honeymoon. She lay on the sand, trying to remember why her husband had hated it.

Through the cotton, his hand felt warm and comforting – like the touch of a father. She put her hand over his hand to keep him there.

"What does a pregnant woman look like?" she asked. It sounded like a riddle, or the beginning of a joke.

"Half asleep," he said. "She has a stillness you do not possess, a cloud over the eyes, like a fish sleeping."

"How do you know what sleeping fish look like?"

"I know."

Franny showered and dressed in one of his shirts, and took the glass of wine he gave her. He kept white wine in his fridge, even though he himself didn't drink. He had made a resolution about drinking. It was one of those decisions about his life for which there was no explanation. The blinds were drawn, and the sun had turned the room brown through the slats. It was very hot in his room, the glass so cold; Franny drank from it.

They made love easily. She cried out when she came, and her cry startled him, for he stopped suddenly and asked if he was hurting her.

No, she managed, using the broken language of lovers.

He lay on his back in a softened mood. She saw bruise-like marks on his body. He told her he had once been a welder. He described the pain in his eyes whenever he had accidentally stared at the flame too long. It was a pain that came to life only hours later, would begin toward evening and increase steadily into the night. There was nothing he could do for it, he said, except cold tea bags. He always kept wet tea bags in his fridge.

Franny started to cry. Not for the pain, for his description of the pain – an insidious pain that only announced itself after the damage was done. He picked her up and carried her to a chair and sat with her on his knee.

"What will I do? What am I going to do?"

"With your life, you mean, or the next minute?"

"What will I do?"

He kissed her.

"Have you ever considered keeping your baby, if it turns out to be real?"

"Why do you want to be with me? I'm no fun to be with."

"I want to be with you," he said simply.

"Tell me what you most don't like about me."

"I like everything about you," he said.

"There must be something. My eyebrows? My voice?"

"I love your voice."

"My husband hated my voice."

There was a silence. It settled between them.

"Has it ever occurred to you that maybe you were never the woman he thought he wanted, that maybe he didn't know what he wanted?"

"It didn't have to turn out the way it did. I loved him, you know." She felt foolish, telling that to a lover.

He gave her a hug and patted her back.

"What will I do? What am I going to do?"

"Stay," he said, "and figure it out." He made her smile, then: "You want tea bags for those eyes?"

He became necessary. He was always there, someone else, someone with his own separate and impenetrable world. He asked nothing of her. There were the days she did not see him, and then the days she did. The days he said he could not see her, she imagined all sorts of things. She imagined he was a prisoner out on parole. The thought that he might once have done something violent frightened her, though she felt certain he would never hurt her.

"I didn't know until yesterday that I would miss you," she said to him one day.

They had rolled up their jeans and waded out to a rock off Second Beach to watch the setting sun. The incoming tide drew an ever-closer ring around them on the rock. Across the harbour, strings of coloured lights suddenly lit the masts of the tall ships moored there.

"Will you miss me when I'm gone?"

"I can take care of myself," he said.

"Can you?"

"Can *you*?" he answered, and she was startled by the edge in his voice.

Franny had spent the day earlier wandering around China Town, buying gifts for her family against her return. Sooner or later, she would have to return. She had just left a bakery carrying a box of assorted pastries when, across the street, she thought she'd seen him waiting for the light to change. He was with a woman. She started to run. She crushed the box of pastries against the old lady blocking her path. A horn screamed at the intersection. She grabbed his forearm and spun him around. There wasn't even a resemblance. She had to lean against a building to catch her breath, tears filling the whole moons of her eyes. She felt sickened. It had not even occurred to her that he might betray her in that way.

"I wasn't in China Town yesterday."

"I'm glad," she said. "You were with a woman."

"It isn't anything like that."

From across the water, they heard the low mournful whistle of a train. It was strangely beckoning. The tide was forcing them from their rock, which, anyway, had begun to grow cold.

"Is *he* what is forcing you back?" he asked, finally.

They always began their evening walks through districts that would remind her of her childhood, around corner stores and down laneways, where as a kid she might have hunted Popsicle sticks and pop bottles. They would end up in a restaurant, for he insisted on feeding her. This one had plastic grapes hanging from the ceiling along with last year's Christmas decorations. They decided on a pizza, while the owner went next door to buy the soft drinks they had ordered. They pumped the jukebox full of quarters and pressed buttons at random, laughing at Neapolitan love songs followed by Elvis Presley. Franny wanted to dance. There was no one else in the restaurant. But in this he would not oblige her. "Please," he said, looking alarmed, as she tried to pull him to his feet.

Midsummer night, they went swimming.

"You'll leave me suddenly," he said, "you'll leave me without warning. You won't leave me enough memories."

They had taken a shortcut through a schoolyard, their wet bathing suits rolled in the same towel. Lovers for three weeks, they were both three weeks behind on their laundry. When she'd told him, "I can't see you tonight, I have to do my laundry," he had said, "Bring it over here, and we'll do it together." "Are you serious," she said, "my dirty underwear spinning around in there with yours?"

Their bathing suits would leave a humid little patch on the wood bleacher when they were gone. They sat together and gazed at the moon. She said, "Let's plan to meet someday in Barcelona."

"We will never meet in Barcelona. One of us will arrive too soon or too late, at the wrong corner, the wrong night…"

He wanted to take her to the market. They would buy a whole salmon and he would show her how to make *gravlox*. If she could wait until late August, they might take a holiday together. They could hike into the mountains and pitch a tent beside a lake, or he would rent a cabin if she preferred. There were so many things still to do yet.

"You're not leaving me with enough memories. We haven't made enough memories."

On the night of fireworks at English Bay, Franny had a fever. For more than a week now she had been waking with a weight on her chest, her throat constricted and flaming. He listened to the symptoms, and then he said, "You have homesickness. In your mind, you are already leaving me." He wrapped her in a sweater, even though it was July. He made a cup of tea and brought it out to her on the balcony, with two aspirins. She took the aspirins in her palm. They were very small and pink. She sat on the chair next to him, with her legs over his, watching the crowds converge toward the bay. He bent over and kissed her knees. He said he loved the smell of her knees, like two sweet flowers. Then he reached over and folded her in. He kissed her deeply. She did not want him to kiss her that way, because of her sore throat. She turned her mouth away. He crushed an aspirin and sprinkled its powder onto her tongue, stroked her neck as she swallowed. He kissed her again.

They made love quickly. He looked down to where she curled under him like a small burning animal. He just looked at her. "What?" she said. He just looked at her, as if memorizing her face.

Fireworks began exploding, shattering the warm blackness into a thousand stars. Each wave caught a glint of it and disbursed light, a handful of stars, so that they were surrounded by a galaxy. Franny felt as if two hands had taken hold of something in her chest and were squeezing it, ever so slightly. With each gentle pressure, she lost her breath. He held her. He held *onto* her, as if he were afraid she might slip under and drown; he might lose her in the black space between lights. While she gazed up at the fireworks, he looked down at her face. "Oh, look," she said. "Yes, look at you," he said. But the rest was lost in a wonder of star-bursts.

That night, he broke silence. Like the closed anemone, he suddenly opened. He told her he had a son.

"Why didn't you tell me sooner?"

"I am telling you now."

"Now is too late."

"I'm glad it's too late."

"It's as if you had lied to me. Why didn't you tell me?"

"You were always going," he said. "I always knew you would leave me in the end. There never seemed to be any point."

"Why now, then? What has made the difference?"

He said nothing. He looked away. He looked like a man condemned, waiting.

What will you do, if it turns out to be real? Have you ever considered keeping your baby?

"Hold me," his child demands, whose father has never asked anything of her, who makes no demands.

Franny makes an armchair of her body, in the shallow waters of English Bay, and lets her chin come to rest on his son's wet little shoulder, to see the waves as the child sees them, to see if he will let her – his dad's new friend, a stranger. What choice does he have? He is just four years old and this is his first time in the ocean, and she thinks what little courage he has to face the waves alone, how he paws the air behind him for her with his fierce little hands. Franny puts her arms around his waist and makes a shell of her body. From his height, the waves have been so huge and darkening, and for an hour now, have been too much. And he wants back to the shore, and once there he wants the ocean again, and when she gives the ocean back to him, he is sick on his excitement and yearns for the shore.

"Fickle," his father says, "like his mother."

"You shouldn't say that. He hears, you know. He will never forget."

"Kick," Franny shouts. "Kick hard and ride with it." The boy stiffens and pulls his little chicken's breast out of the water, hanging from her hands. Her back aches with his new weight. He shrieks ecstatically as he bicycles over the next wave, thinking he did it all on his own. Like his father. *Like his father.*

Throughout the afternoon, older women have smiled, and Franny smiles back, accepting a guilty maternity. There is a man on the shore – a man who knows, who has been watching her all afternoon.

"Why don't you take off your dark glasses and come in?" The child's questions give everything away. Franny is wearing a green and yellow kerchief wrapped around her hair, to match the green bathing suit. She keeps her head above the water.

"I am *in*, sweetheart."

"No you're not."

The child still has not looked at her.

For some reason, his father has not brought his bathing suit. Franny sends him back to the apartment to fetch it. His son's first swim in the ocean. This is too important to miss. They promise to wait the twenty minutes out on the sand. She will not let his son swim in the ocean. Together they will sit on this towel, she promises. She will teach the boy how to build sandcastles, while they wait for his father to come back.

The child kicks sand with his heel. He edges away from the towel, pushing the limits. There is no containing him. He is picking a wet string of seaweed from the sand and shaking it out like a tail. Anxiously, she seeks his father on the shore. The next moment a wave has flattened him, the boy who is more shocked than harmed, has only swallowed some water. She sweeps him up in her arms. His face has gone alarmingly blank, emptied almost, and then the whole weight of the day crests in a soul-shattering scream. She watches him turn red, little ribs pumping, face pulled into one convulsive knot. Just as suddenly, the sound stops, displaced by that unearthly stillness she finds so disturbing in his father.

"He's had enough," his father says. He stands beside them.

Franny is suddenly so tired she wants only to lie down, to curl up on the sand, to let the sun bake her.

"Tell me something," she says.

"Stay," he says, "don't go yet."

Franny leaves them shaking sand out of their towels, and walks to the women's change house. The man who has been watching her all afternoon looks up as she passes. He grins, as if to say, *I've got your number*. Franny stares at him murderously and the eyes slide away.

"Down, Daddy, please… please, Daddy."

They have caught up to her, the boy dressed hastily in a T-shirt and white sunhat, bouncing helplessly on his father's shoulders, clutching his dad's hair, while the father, slung with towels and running-shoes and cameras and pants, secures him by an arm across the ankles. They look like a ship under full sail, the ropes and canvas not fully battened.

She touches his arm. The ship comes to rest.

"You don't like it up there, do you, sweetheart?"

"No." It is almost too quiet.

"So what do we do now? Would you both like some ice cream?"

"Let him down," Franny says, "He's miserable up there."

He lets the boy scramble down from his shoulders. The son stands apart from them, at an unforgiving little distance. Not a twitch. It is as if one move might draw attention to himself and land him right back up on his father's shoulders.

"So what do we do now?" the father says uncertainly.

Franny stares at the back of the little white sunhat, and presses her forehead with her palm. "I need shade," she says, "let's find a tree."

They are sitting on a park bench beneath the great outspreading branches of a tree, and Franny is so grateful for its green, for its solidity, she has an impulse to reach out and pat its bark. They sit facing the street. Bone-weary, is she, with an ache in her back that seems pulling her to earth. It suddenly occurs to her that the boy is not moving, not tugging at anything, not running off to be fetched back. He is just sitting there along with them, facing the street.

"You see that bus stop?" his father explains, "he thinks we're waiting for a bus."

Franny bursts out laughing.

"Do you mean that's all you have to do to get him to stay still? Find a bus stop and *pretend* to be waiting?"

She had been waiting for a bus when she met him. He'd had a cup of coffee in one hand, and had taken sips from a hole he had poked through the lid. He had looked relaxed, a newspaper tucked comfortably under an arm. She was furious at having just missed the bus, at the prospect of the wait. He had watched her pace. "You're from out of town," he had said. "After living on the coast for a while, you'll develop webbed feet. You won't take waiting so seriously."

"So what do we do now?"

Now, they were waiting. They were, all three of them, waiting. The boy was waiting for the bus. His father was waiting for Franny. And she was waiting for... something. She didn't know what.

"I have to buy my train ticket today."

The train station is like something in a dream. There are so many people, all trying to leave town, and nothing available on any of the days she thought to travel.

"I don't believe I am doing this," he says, as he dials the number for CN, the alternate route. For some reason Franny has not been able to get through; she keeps dialling the wrong number.

"Doesn't it tell you something?" he says, "or aren't you listening?"

"So I'll get a ticket for the first available day, or I'll go by coach and not a sleeper. Nothing says I have to leave on a Saturday or Sunday, or any other day of the week. I have nothing to hold me."

He hangs up the phone and catches her. "Am I nothing?" As suddenly as the tears start, they have stopped. She wipes her face on his shirt and looks around for the son. The boy is keeping his usual respectful distance, his back to them both.

"Didn't even notice," she says, and laughs uncomfortably.

"Don't fool yourself," he says, "the little smartass sees everything."

An hour later, they come back to the spot where Franny has been waiting in line. The boy runs up to her, holding out his new rubber snake.

"And what do we have here, sweetheart?"

"We had hamburgers," the boy tells her.

"So is it done?" his father asks, grimly.

"Are you coming to Nanny's with us?" the boy asks, throttling his snake. She bends down at the knees and holds herself in a cannonball.

"If it's all the same to you, sweetheart, I think I'll wait outside on the sidewalk."

"Don't be silly," the father says, and grabs one hand from each. "How much time do I have?" he asks savagely. "How much time to change your mind?"

"It won't be changed," she tells him. "We have a week."

On the bus to Nanny's Franny teaches the boy how to play "this-little-piggy-went-to-market," only his little piggies prefer spaghetti to roast beef.

"I didn't know you knew those kind of games," he says. "I never would have thought it of you." Franny wonders how he perceives her. He is sitting on the aisle-seat, legs crossed, arm around them both, making a moon-curve of his body.

"I was a kid once, you know," Franny tells him. "I have a mother."

The boy's little fist bores into her stomach, support-ing the whole of his window-gazing weight. She covers the fist with her hand.

To look at them, you might think they were a family coming home from the beach, sunburnt and spent.

"Where's his hat?" the father asks suddenly.

The child says nothing. His neck stiffens. Franny sees the blond hairs bristle above his sunburn.

"His mother bought it?" she asks.

"You know what this'll look like – like I haven't been watching, like I don't care…"

When they get off the bus, the child bolts in the direction of a grocery store. His father lets go of Franny's hand.

A woman is bent down beside a fruit stand, holding out a peeled banana, listening to what the child has to say. Whatever it is, he is telling it wildly. As they approach, the chatter stops. Her eyes move from the child to his father, and then to Franny.

"I've heard so much about you," she says. Franny is dismayed to think that while she knew nothing of this woman, her lover's mother has heard all about her.

"You are on holiday?" she asks. "Will you come back, do you think?"

"I don't know. At this stage in my life, I don't know that I want to repeat any experience."

"Even good ones?" the mother asks. She glances at her son, and in her glance Franny sees a mother's worry.

The child tugs at Franny's dress. He is trying to draw her away from the circle of adults, to tell her something. His little face is knotted with the effort. He takes her hand, and pulls her out into the yard. It seems his snake is caught up in the tree. As Franny reaches up into the branches, her stomach cramps with the unmistakable pain of her period.

It had been a masked pregnancy, he had married the boy's mother too young.

Franny asked what that meant – "masked pregnancy."

He said it happens when the mother denies to herself that she is pregnant, despite the growing signs. When his wife's labour had come, she was in a state of complete panic. It was as if she didn't know what was happening. She hadn't wanted to go to the hospital. She believed she had the stomach flu.

"I blame myself," he said. "I blame myself, for not really helping her."

Within a week of the birth, she had disappeared. She had checked herself out of the hospital, and then taken the baby with her. It took him nine months to find the son – nine months of his son's life he knew nothing about. And then came the legal battles with the Children's Aid Society.

"What happened to her? What happened to your wife?"

"She committed suicide," he said quietly. "She was only nineteen."

That was all he would say.

He said he had known all along that Franny wasn't pregnant.

"How do you explain, then, the three-month absence of my period?"

"It was a false pregnancy. You wanted his baby. You still love him and don't know it. That's why you're going back."

Franny felt her face burn. She wanted to hit him. "That's not true," she said. "It's a lie." She hit him in the chest.

"You tell me," he said.

He planted a hand on either side of her and caged her within his arms. He forced her legs apart with his knee. She felt something turn over in her, a deep excitement between her ribs.

"Don't forget me," he said. "Don't forget you're coming back."

That night Franny had a dream. Her mother came to her by train. They met on a dark night, between cars. She held a box in her hands. Franny could not hear what her mother was trying to say to her. The squeal of metal drowned out the words. Lights flashed across her face. Her face was full of a mother's love, and something else – a strange new fear. They did not kiss or embrace. Their meeting was coldly unemotional. She had come all that way and Franny did not even kiss her. Her mother placed the box in her hands and sadly withdrew. Franny knew that in the box was her unborn baby.

On their last night, he took her to a Portuguese restaurant. It was called *Le Fado*. He told her that a *fado* is a sad song a sailor sings for his country, missing his home.

"You made my summer," he said. "I know this hasn't been a very good summer for you."

He was sitting back in his chair, a little distant from her. His arms were folded across his chest. His body looked relaxed. The body of her lover. Strong and quiet. He was letting her go.

It was the first time he dreamt of her, he said – a sign that in a way she had already left. In his dream, a tree was burning in the corner of the living room. It was burning from inside. He could see this through a fissure in its bark. He took a sheet from his bed and began to wrap it around the trunk, thinking to smother the flames. But as he bound the tree, he felt the heat grow fiercer. He had to unwind the sheet to take a second look. Through the crack, he saw flames turning the whole inside to white ash. It must have been burning like that for the longest time. He realized he would have to take an axe and cut through to where it burned, to put it out from inside. But how could he, without felling the whole tree? He had understood, then, he could do nothing for the tree.

"I woke knowing the fire was your love for him, and that you, somehow, were the tree."

He took Franny's hand. He turned it over and laid a kiss in the palm. He looked down at the palm and touched it with his fingers, as if to see if his kiss had left any impression.

"You don't have a lifeline," he said, looking up at her in surprise.

"That's ridiculous," she said, "I'm here, aren't I?"

"Are you, Franny? Were you ever here? Sometimes your love felt like something I intercepted."

Franny looked away. She felt ashamed. She had wanted him to love her, *needed* it, selfishly, for herself – to cancel out that another had not. She felt responsible for this.

"Once," she began, "I sat in on one of his math classes. He taught at the university. I wanted to surprise him, to watch him at his work. For a whole hour we were in the same room together, without his ever once seeing me. When the class was over I went up to him. I stood among the students near his desk. He looked right at me, without seeing me, as if I weren't there. Did it happen, I wonder? Or was it just something I imagined? It made my whole life seem tenuous."

He shifted in his seat, imagining her there, seeing her face waiting to surprise another man.

"When I left him, he never called. Not even once. Not even to ask why. It was as if we had never been married. I lied to you about that, about seeing him before I left. I didn't have to run away. He would never have come after me... Don't hate me," she said finally, "I have to go home."

Silence. His low voice. "I know," he said.

"I just wanted you to know."

They agreed not to have any train-station parting. They agreed not to write. "There must be some reality to our relationship," he said. But no sooner was she tasting prairie dust than she had written her first letter, and there was a letter waiting for her when she got home:

"It has been two days since I saw you and it seems as if you are just around the corner somewhere, but I just haven't stumbled around that right corner yet. It's a feeling of helplessness. You were here, and then gone, and nothing is the same since you left. Today, riding on the bus down Hastings past your old stop, there was a girl walking – slender, with long hair swinging down her back. It embarrasses me to say that my heart skipped a beat. I almost choked. Back to my senses before the bus passed, I strained to see her face. She was nothing like you. Do I see you everywhere? Or is it, as I fear, that I am already forgetting? And when *will* I see you again? For I must see you again, Franny. I must…"

She had wanted to comfort him: "There was this corner, where I stood, not long after my return to the east, waiting for the light to change." What happened there?

It had changed. It had changed again, and still Franny had stood, not crossing the street. Then she had stepped sideways and into a phone booth. She hadn't answered his *hello,* listening instead to the voice of a wailing baby in his background. *He has a child – already,* she had thought, of the husband who had not sought after her, who had not waited for her return. It was as if she had been waiting on that corner, forever, while he had gone on and was miles and miles ahead of her. *And now you are behind me,* she had wanted to tell him, her man of the west, but did not. *Now I know that waiting is a kind of grieving. It comes before the thing you are waiting to die is actually dead.* She had stepped out of the booth and off that corner.

The letters that followed were constant in their tone. They were even, and tender, and wise. A new voice had begun to emerge in them. He spoke of things with wry humour. Whenever Franny read his letters she thought of his laugh, the way he had laughed with his chin tucked into his chest. This was not that laughter.

They were two months into writing letters when he said he was coming east. He would be whatever she wanted. He would be lover, or husband, or friend. She had only to say the word. But Franny was afraid. *And what if I say "yes" and he doesn't come? What if these are only words, in a letter? And if the words were truly meant, why wouldn't he simply show up?* She wrote and asked him not to come.

A year went by without a letter. When she wrote again, it was a few words on a Christmas card. With what joy she found the letter that followed in her mail slot. In the letter, he spoke of a journey he had made with his son, "the little squirt, now grown into a back-talking little prick," he wrote with fatherly affection. They had "cruised across country" in one of the wide-tracking Pontiacs he said he was "wheeling about with these days." He had taken his son back to see the hospital where he had been born. Franny understood that her lover was making peace with his past, with a young mother's suicide, with himself, was leaving all this behind, back where it belonged, a long time ago, now. She felt a fierce surge of release, not so much of freedom but escape, and at the same time, seared to the core by an almost sexual grief, as when he withdrew that first time, without ever coming. Surely she had never been so wondrously, so almost in love.

On her knees before the raised hearth of the sunken living room where now she lives, she is on her knees, cleaning out ashes with a bronze fire iron. As Franny reaches to remove one log's remains, she feels a hot pain from palm to heart. *Forgive me, as I forgive you.* She sees his eyes, bleached by the acetylene flames of fabrication, the eyes of her almost love, alone in the shop where he fabricates, alone and still waiting. *Did I let it die, or did you let me go? And why is it that we did that?* Palms to forehead, her eyes closed, impressed now with ashes, she sits back on her haunches, before the fireplace, where last night she had stared at the flames too long, unable to move. She presses down hard against her closed eyes until veins of light explode in the darkness behind her lids. Then she releases her palms, gets up off her knees, and goes…

Linda Rogers

DARLING BOY

I didn't feel a thing. Hair doesn't have feelings. Not even red hair. Not even when I'm stoned. Especially when I'm stoned; and that's an important detail because the cop who went to the Cop Oscars for arresting that famous bank robber dragged me all the way up the cliff from Mile Zero by my ponytail the night me and my buddies got busted for hanging at the beach.

I'm a ginger and that means hard to stone, hard to put out for surgery, but easy to piss off.

But I'm not. Pissed at Daisy. Fair is fair. I have all the advantages. I can remember the magic numbers to get in and out. I get to choose the books we read and the food that I eat. Daisy just got it in her head she wanted some kind of keepsake, snuggled up close as if to see the pictures in the book about Wounded Knee and, gotcha, I was missing some ginger and she was dancing inside a circle of Dementia-Girls whooping like Sitting Bull's warriors. Lucky I was wearing my magic shirt full of roach holes that never burned me. Who knows, she might've thought of hacking off some skin.

"Where'd you get these?" I put down our book, got up, disarmed her gently, and brought her back to her chair. Daisy doesn't need scissors. People come in to fix her hair and her nails. The nurses chop up her food. She put her handful of my crowning glory in her pocket with a smirk I would never call a smile. It was pure naughty.

"No more ghost stories," I warned her. "They give you bad ideas."

"You mad at me?" She grabbed my hand and kissed the fish webbing between my fingers. Ginger on speed, they said, before I quit swimming. How many husbands did she waste? Daisy can charm the seeds out of a nickel bag.

"I'm mad about you," she said, half-singing so I knew it was an old tune. Daisy is a human jukebox. I wish I had half that number of songs in my head.

Matt, the physio, says we're an item. That's a relief to him because all the other ladies stalk him. It started when he asked the Dees to make like they're windshield wipers and she couldn't get her arms going in opposite directions.

"Unison's good," I said, and we did it together. That got her laughing.

"She never laughs," Matt said, and that was how I got off janitor duty and became her special reader, even after my hundred hours were up. We have a connection. She calls me Darling Boy because she can't remember my name. That's OK by me. When you're a ginger with your name on the cop blotter, anonymity is a true endorphin hit.

Daisy does remember some things. Unison got her going. Her brain is wired for opera. A nurse gave her earphones so she could listen in private; but she sings along, and we all try to get through it without wetting ourselves, especially when she dances. She's dem bones dancing.

I like reggae myself. Daisy made a face when I downloaded a bunch of tunes, but she did get up and shake her moneymaker, or the handful of skin that's left of it. Matt laughed his face off.

"You got her number all right."

"She's got mine too." I make like I'm dialling up the lonely muscle on the left side of my rib cage. Daisy is cool with me and she never tells me to do my home-work, go to school, cut my hair or quit smoking ganja. That would be my business. I've taken charge of my life and I have a new family, all friends, and no blood rela-tions.

In a way, it was her idea to get me working with the dementia team. One morning when I was still chipping off my hours with a broom, I found her redecorating the day room, moving the chairs around. You've got to know, some of those chairs, especially the La-Z-Boys, are heavy and she's small lady. Just to give you a pic-ture, I'll tell you she's about a hand span over five feet tall and she eats as much as an ant can carry in one load. Daisy wears yellow and she smells like dandelions. Even when she's just had her hair done, she wears a sunhat with fake flowers stuck in the band.

"Awesome, you're a monster," I said, watching her motorize chairs, wondering what she was on. "What's up?"

"We need a meeting." Daisy wasn't even puffed out. This is the lady who calls her visits to the washroom "hikes."

"What about?"

"You know," she said, one of her two standard answers. One is "You know" and the other is "Sometimes yes, and sometimes no." Either way she avoids making mistakes. I think she is way more with it than she gets credit for. I should have answered like that at school. They might've thought I was Einstein throwing the questions back at them.

"No, I don't."

She let go of the chair she was scraping across the linoleum ("It's got to be linoleum because some of the girls pee themselves," she'd confided) and whispers, "We're all prisoners here. They won't let us back into Canada. It isn't fair. We're Canadians."

"You're right," I said "It isn't."

"So we're going to have a revolution," she announced, Daisy proud of Daisy for dialling the right word that time.

"Oh." That's what I got for reading her stories about Che, Louis Riel and Sitting Bull. Back in Canada, I'm willing to bet she voted Conservative but in Deeland, Daisy's gone rogue. I wondered if I should sneak in a joint. It might help with her constipation.

"You have to help."

"What am I going to do?" At this point in my life I feel I've got as much potential as ice cubes in hell.

"You're going to make a speech."

"A speech? Me? What about?"

"You're going to tell them."

"Tell them what?"

"To let us out and in."

"Where?"

"Canada. We want in. It's our right."

"You've got to give me some time."

I noticed the Dees had put away their blank expressions, which only happens when little kids and dogs come into the ward. They were smiling and winking at me. Daisy really had them worked up, which was neat but it totally maxed my stress level. This could land me in jail, which I barely avoided last time I stuck my red head up. Jail scares the crap out of me. I've heard ginger boys get the egg beater where the sun doesn't shine if they step out of line; and who decides where the line is anyway?

"OK. I'll make a speech tomorrow." And maybe I'll never come back, I thought.

Soon as I got out of there, I lit up a doobie and walked around the hospital hood. It was spring and (they don't call Victoria the Garden City for nothing) colour saturated, like being in a Johnny Depp movie. Daisy loves her garden walks. Isn't that Canada enough for one old lady?

The trippy gardens handed me a plan. The deck off the day room is big enough to have a name and there was nothing growing in the planters, somebody's great idea gone to waste. I knew what to do.

Daisy hadn't forgotten. Soon as I walked in with my big garbage bag she and her ladies crowded around me like hens at feeding time (I know this because I used to look after the chickens at our farm). I have to admit the dementia ladies *smell* like a henhouse.

"Well?" she asked, white knuckles gripping her hip-bones.

"OK," I said. "Back off, ladies. Follow me. We're going to Canada." I led them to the door.

"Canada?" she said, when they were all outside on the deck.

"Yes. Inside is purgatory." (I know that word from my brief incarceration at Sunday school). "Outside is Canada." I let them peek in my bag. "I have some plant donations."

From that moment, everything changed. We planted and weeded. The Dees, God's gaga gardeners, got high on flowers. When the days got shorter, we had a great Indian summer and the petunias, marguerites, geraniums and pansies I got with the five-finger discount sailed into fall with all their flags flying.

Most days, the ladies stayed outside in Canada and fussed over their plants. When it rained, Daisy cranked up her headset and danced in the day room, and they boogied with her, waving their watering cans. Could've been a zombie jamboree.

"You believe in zombies?" I asked Matt.

"I believe everything I see, brother."

"I think there is life after death."

"You might be right."

"Maybe reincarnation. My mother tells me I'm going to come back as a cockroach."

"Could be worse." He moved off with his smooth smile and a basket of squeezie balls for arthritis exercises, leaving me with my cranky criminal, wondering what worse might be.

"You shouldn't have cut my hair, Daisy. It's a boundary violation. I have an OC problem: No wrinkles in my bed and every hair in place." I patted my head to make the point.

She wasn't listening and her eyes were 100 percent pupil, black holes of forgetfulness you wouldn't want to fall into. If I didn't know better, I'd say she'd had a bad dose. Just when I peered into the void, she reached right in my pocket and clawed back the scissors. Then she took off for Canada.

I got up real slow. I was afraid to run after her in case she tripped and fell on the blades. Freaky samurai. Read the headline, "Ginger Stalks Sweet Old Lady With Scissors."

While I was walking on eggs, the Dees lined up at the window. It was lunchtime, but they were more interested in watching Daisy snip. Who cared if the soup got cold? By the time I tiptoed close enough to hear what she was saying, she'd ripped off half the petals, "He loves me / He loves me not."

"Give me the scissors, please." I put my hand out.

"He loves me not." She shouted, "Off with their heads," and I didn't know what to do. Daisy was fully armed and I was scared to death she was going to hurt herself. Snip. Snip. Petals fell like infantry.

At the picture windows, the Dees clapped and cheered, their mouths and eyes as blank and psycho as the characters in Japanese comics. This gave her more energy. She was a human smart bomb, taking everything down.

"Please."

"Party's over," Matt said. He came up so quietly behind her, his white hospital shoes could've been moccasins.

"You're damn right." Daisy turned, handed over her weapon of mass destruction and announced, "Time for a time out."

Matt put her hand in the crook of his elbow and guided her down the hall, singing, *"Daisy, Daisy, give me your answer do,"* but she wasn't having any of it. She stuck out her foot and delivered all two hundred pounds of Matt meat straight to the floor. He didn't see it coming. The Dees, afraid of reprisals, I guess, an extra dose of the prune goo, poo on a spoon, after lunch, slunk toward the dining room and I stayed put.

"Give her time," Matt said when he came back, limping slightly but looking brave. "They're serving shrimp salad sandwiches with the soup. She loves shrimp day."

I knew what he meant. Like a dog, Daisy can smell chocolate in my pocket.

"OK. I'll give it a couple of days." It was time for me to shuffle off to the candy store. Daisy'd hid a twenty in my book before she cut me. The Dees aren't supposed to give us tips, but it wasn't for me, not all of it. She rewards me for bringing in contraband. Daisy has a sweet tooth, but she isn't allowed candy because of the diabetes. Heck, she's ninety. Why not die happy with a wad of toffee stuck to your false teeth?

Reprisal time, I got high on her dime and ate most of the candy myself and now, after waiting three days, I'm dropping in with a bag of gummy bears and a new library book, *The Edge of Physics,* a journey to Earth's extremes to unlock the secrets of the universe. That should challenge both of us. I can't even pronounce the writer's last name.

Zippety doo dah, it's an awesome morning. When I punch in my numbers and tiptoe into the day room (I was going to come up behind her and put my hands over her eyes), Daisy's nowhere to be seen. I look out the window at Canada and she isn't there either. There are no new faces on the flowers. It looks like the grim reaper's been out there.

"Where's Daisy?" I ask, but the Dementia Ladies give me their who-are-you looks. I undertake a search.

She's in her room. Matt is sitting beside her bed, one of her manicured hands in his brown one, the other gripping the keepsake she took without permission.

"It's closing time," he says. "Daisy's decided." He says this like she still gets to and lets me take it all in for a minute: the stuffed animals, the dead violets, the black-and-white photos on her table, and Our Lady of the Deadheads herself, lying there quiet and pale.

"She got into bed after you left the other day and she's refusing to eat or drink. Not your fault. This is what they do when they're done."

Then we're quiet. I hear rubber soles in the hall and shallow breathing. The nurses come by and take her pulse. One of them shows me the blood pooling at her knees and I notice her toenails are painted bright pink. Day turns into night. After forever, I hear Daisy go

"Oh!" letting go of a surprised little puff of air, and Matt stands up.

"Time's up," he says, stretching, watching with me as her fingers stiffen around the curl she stole.

He gives me a big man hug and says, "Her son was a redhead, Darling Boy."

Daniel Perry

MERCY

1

In Waubnakee, we don't have a pitcher's mound. The base paths aren't lined, and the infield's not grass. The Superintendent drives out from Currie once a spring, to roll the gravel flat, and you'd think he cuts the out-field just as often. We like the Jays fine, but on summer nights we live for softballs wheeled underhand, rising the forty feet from pitcher to batter, and the aluminum ping of long drives over four-man outfields, displacing the humidity and the whirring mosquitoes while in the canteen, sultry Jessie Mueller roasts hot dogs and pouts, "What can I do *you* for?"

Mothers in Waubnakee use her as the example. I heard my own in our yard, yesterday, bawling out my sister for hanging shirts on the clothesline by the shoul-ders. "It stretches out the neck!" she yelled from the back door. "You think Jessie Mueller's got it bad? Just you *try* dressing like that, Missy, tits hanging out for the whole town to see. *I* won't pick you up at the police sta-tion."

It's a natural leap for Mom, and it has been since she got into Ray Tarkington's Mustang on a Friday in August, 1977. Ray's father drove that car to London two months later and pushed his son out at Wolesley Barracks; from there the army shipped him to Gagetown, New Brunswick. I was born the next spring, on a Sunday, just before the Men's League game. Mom says the Wanderers missed Ray that year, and finished last in the Township. He came home on leave when I was two and married Mom, but when she got pregnant with Nancy he left again, for good, via telephone. John Carrion moved in before Nancy was born. He was just twenty, the same age as Mom. Nancy and I know he's not our father, but we call him "Dad." He's done more for us than Ray ever did.

Hank Mueller, Jessie's bearded, beer-bellied father, replaced Ray as cleanup hitter. "Your old boy could hit the ball a mile," he told me once, in front of Dad, of course, staring at him and challenging him. "I even seen him put it *on the road* one time," he said, which *is* pretty far – provided that it actually happened. But if anyone would know, it was Hammerin' Hank, who got the nickname like Greenberg and Aaron for his bat, and for the one time he chased a boyfriend of Jessie's off his property with a twelve-pound sledge. We look over our shoulders before we say it.

Hank drives tow truck for a living, and three springs ago he bought Dad's beloved blue pickup after dragging it home from Highway 401. He told Dad the truck needed a new motor, but really the problem was a three-dollar valve, and the truck was back on the road in a month, just in time for Jessie and me to graduate Grade Eight. While I was on stage being handed the English Award, Jessie was sneaking out the back door of the gym with the spare key she had swiped from her mom's purse. She drove the truck to a high-school bush party. Hank charged Jessie with theft, and the judge gave her community service. That's why she makes hot dogs now.

er

Jessie and I have sisters the same age, too, thirteen. Hers are twins, Rebecca and Stacey, and they're tall and athletic and already assured a spot on *senior* volleyball when they start at Currie High School this fall.

Nancy is chubby and has dirty blond hair. She played one season of soccer when she was seven, and after three games it ended with a goal post and a broken tooth. Now she likes to read books about flying insects and she wanders around our backyard identifying them. So this morning, when Mom took her to register for Waubnakee's first girls' softball team, I knew something was up.

Beyond the outfield fence, chain link and topped with black tile, the plaque on the shed-sized Currie

Township Museum says the town's been here two hundred years. And the population records inside show that there has always been enough girls eleven to thirteen to field a squad. But all around the room, where the walls join the ceiling, photos of Waubnakee's most accomplished women cast judgment through bright tacky eye-shadow. Fall Fair Princesses give way to Homemaking Queens, who keep watch over the *pièce de resistance*, the Waubnakee Recipe Archive. So are teenage girls in Waubnakee suddenly into softball? No. Not remotely. There's one legit job in town – at Jack McCann's ValuGas, evenings, five-to-ten – and I've got it. Everyone else works down the highway in London, or at least as far as Currie, and no one's parents get home before eight.

A month ago, the Mueller twins missed the bus from Currie Elementary and rode home in a twelfth-grader's Camaro. He was lucky to drop them off while Hank was on a call. When word got out, parents said, "Boys will be boys," but they must have called a meeting, and they must have chosen softball. What scares them most is girls being girls.

er

I quit playing ball when I started at ValuGas, and most nights I watch the Blue Jays on the little rabbit-eared TV beside the till. We lock the pumps when the

Wanderers play, on Tuesday nights and long weekend Sundays, and we tape a battered note to the door that says *AT THE BALL PARK. COME GET US IF YOU NEED GAS.*

We've never missed a pitch.

Tonight, a Friday, I show up early and ask Jack, "Do you mind staying?" I've played catch with Nancy in our yard all week, in the hour between school and work, and her first practice is about to start. "I promised my sister I'd come watch," I say. "She's afraid everyone will laugh at her."

Jack tucks his grey hair behind his ears, under his green Seedcorp mesh-back, and he chuckles. He bends to open the cabinet below the register and I hear him tear off new tape. He produces the note and says, "I'll come too." We follow the gravel lane behind the gas bar to the park, where ten girls sulk on the bleachers in bad pre-teen makeup. Tonight's also the monthly youth dance in Currie – no coincidence – and rides to Centennial Arena's upstairs lounge hinge on going to practice.

From the group of parents milling around the canteen, tanned, smiley Shawn Baylor emerges. He's just over thirty, and he moved here this winter from London, where both of his daughters played. He introduces himself as the coach and leads the girls onto the field. They drag their feet until he sits them on the grass in a half-circle. His oldest, Christine, will be pitcher, he says, and her sister, Samantha – who's only ten – will catch. The rest of the girls sigh in relief. It's short-lived.

"Who wants to play first base?" Shawn asks.

No one volunteers.

He frowns.

"Second?"

Silence.

"How about third?"

No response.

"Well," he says. "You must all be shortstops."

"What's a shortstop?" asks Nancy.

Shawn leans in to close the sale. "It's the best position, between second and third." He smiles. "You'll get a lot of balls hit to you."

"Then no," Nancy says, shaking her head.

"We should put our best athlete there, anyway," he says. "Rebecca. And our other best athlete" – he gestures to Stacey – "in centre field." He assigns the other positions seemingly at random, though Nancy in right field can't be an accident.

The girls partner off along the first-base line and play catch to warm up. Shawn walks from pair to pair and takes one player aside at a time, to demonstrate throws from the shoulder, not the wrist. When he calls away a freckle-faced farm girl named Melissa – Nancy's partner – my sister stands still and looks at the ground, too shy to ask another pair if she can join. She brought my dusty old equipment bag, which sits on the bench now. I walk to the cage and find my glove still inside. The worn leather embraces my fingers like old friends and I jog onto the field. Nancy throws the ball to me and we play like we did in the yard, she dodging my tosses and hers landing well in front of me. Melissa returns, and I throw with her while Shawn talks to Nancy. He continues down the line, and so do I, until he's talked to the last player. He whistles and sends the girls to their positions. I take off my glove and start toward the bleachers. Shawn calls, "Mike! Mind hitting a few?" I shrug and turn toward the bench for a bat. While I splash softballs everywhere but right field – I never could go the other way – Shawn moves around the diamond, talking to each fielder about her role. He becomes the pitcher afterward, and I replace each girl who's in for batting practice, offering the odd tip to my neighbours in the field. They uniformly roll their eyes. The last batter finishes and Shawn ends the practice. The girls all sprint for the parking lot. I walk to the bench and I hand Shawn the bat.

"Think you could come back next week?" he asks.

All the parents may be in on the plan but, apparently, Shawn's the only one coaching. Before I answer, engines rumbling to life startle me. I look toward the parking lot, past right field, past the canteen, where Jessie's lowering the window flap, standing on tiptoes to unlock it for the boys' game, up next. Her long black ponytail brushes her pale shoulders, bare except for two light purple slivers, the straps of her tank top.

I look to Jack, who has caught me staring. He laughs and winks. "The note's got you covered," he says.

er

We expect to lose when we arrive in Currie the next Friday. They have twenty times Waubnakee's population, enough for a Blue team and a White team, even in girls' league. And because only one of them can be the champion, the association gives Blue to the longest-tenured coach, who stacks it. This is the team waiting on the diamond, warming up in matching blue jackets, blue jersey numbers sewn on white sleeves.

Our girls choose yellow, white-screened *Waubnakee* tees by size, Samantha's number 1 the smallest, from a cardboard box in Shawn's minivan moments before the game. When they take the field for the top of the first, Shawn tells me he thought about pink, but that he knew some of the mothers would object. He laughs.

"The goal is to get their minds *off* being pretty," he says.

Blue scores the eight-run limit with ease, and in our half, our batters strike out, one-two-three. In the second, Blue tacks on another seven, putting the score to

15-0. The umpire signals to both coaches, calling off the game.

"Mercy rule," Shawn mutters. He looks at his watch. "Twenty minutes." The parents in the bleachers start grousing about gas money. Shawn waves Blue's coach over, and after a short discussion Waubnakee takes on Blue's back-up pitcher and half of their hitters. We send back our neediest in the hope that they'll soak up some skill and we play out the time limit. In the last inning of the new game, when "Waubnakee" is only down 4-0, Rebecca screams a triple past first base. From third she calls to the next batter, Nancy, "Come on! Hit me home!"

In the Bigs, the call would be the Suicide Squeeze: a bunt toward first to disorient the fielders while the runner on third races home. The Braves tried it in '92 against the Jays, for the Series, but Timlin threw to Carter in time. Nancy puts a full swing on the first pitch and accomplishes the same, a dribbler between the pitcher and first. At the sound of the ping, Rebecca leaves third, and with a head-first slide that looks more like a belly flop she scores. The pitcher stands, ball in hand, watching the play at home, and she turns around too late to throw Nancy out. Our girls scream – even the ones fielding for "Blue" – and they run to the plate to surround Rebecca, our new captain, who rises wincing from the swirling grey dust.

2

ValuGas picks up the last week of July, when the Ritter Pulley plant in Currie closes for maintenance and its workers take their families to Lake Erie. I used to go, too, but now I'm needed close to home, to fill cars and get everyone else out of here. Mom and Dad left tonight for New Highlands, a trailer park in a little beach town called Scotsport, and they took Nancy with them, still in her uniform after Waubnakee's first win, 4-3 over the team from the Reserve. As the Buick pulled away from the diamond, Mom joked "No big parties!" through the window, but she knew I'd have a few friends over for a bonfire. I invited ten, but with most people gone to the lake, the only one I'd bet on is Brian Callaghan, my best friend. I told him to come around eight, so when I walk across the tracks at seven-thirty, his rust-bucket Chev S-10 is already in the yard, doors open, its factory-issue speakers farting out the classic rock station.

Ours is the only house east of the tracks in Waubnakee. The town grew with the railroad until sometime in the thirties, and on our acre lot was once the Reese Hotel, where rail workers lodged between shifts. The librarian at school says other people stayed, too: people who were just passing through, who got out to see the town.

Tourists.

Here.

But in the school's microfiche, the black-and-white *Waubnakee Seed* pictures prove it, chronicling guests up to and including the last, the three masked men who lit the Reese Hotel fire. According to the articles alongside, The Reese was a bootlegging front. And though The Reese had been the first sign of an east side of town, after the fire nothing was built beyond the tracks, save for our house, sometime in the seventies, when it finally replaced the burned-out ruin. Since then, Waubnakee has shrunk to two hundred people, and every night twelfth-graders floor their gas pedals at the stop sign and charge up County Road 17 – Main Street – vaulting the level crossing and rocketing out of town, launching empty beer bottles onto our lawn as they do.

Brian sits on a red cooler as I approach, unfolding a black fibreglass tent pole, and when I turn down my laneway he's just blond buzz-cut and broad shoulders, kneeling on the six-man canvas on the ground. Over The Doors' *Light My Fire* I yell, "Brian!" I hate The Doors. This station plays them every fifteen minutes.

"Just in time," Brian says without looking up. He pushes the pole through its sleeve, the last one, and he motions across the tent. "Grab the other side?"

"I told you, everyone's gone," I say. "There's room in the house." But I walk around the tent anyway and bend down to grasp the fabric. I take one sleeve in each hand and support the tent while he circles it. The poles arc as he secures them in the eyelets. He walks the few feet from the tent to its bag and he pulls out the fly.

"My mom put new sheets on Nancy's bed for you," I say.

Brian laughs and throws the fabric over the tent.

"Come on," he says. "Be a man. It's a beautiful night."

I think of my sleeping bag, stored in the garage, dusty and probably moth-eaten. No one's touched the camping stuff since we got the trailer. Brian walks the circle again, hooking each stretchy cord into its ring.

"No wind tonight," he says. "No need to peg it." We move to the cooler and we each take a side. We set it down at the fire pit at the back of the lot, a rust-covered truck rim in a hole in the ground, and I walk to the woodpile against the wire fence that separates our yard from the cornfield. I take some kindling from the rotting cardboard box and pile it in the centre of the pit. I light it. Mom and Dad sit out here practically every night, and they've left us two lawn chairs folded out. I sit down in one and Brian hands me a beer. His chair creaks and wobbles as he sits down too. He clinks his bottle to mine and we drink.

"How's ball?" he asks.

"The girls got their first win tonight," I say.

Brian laughs.

"I meant your team."

"I told you, I'm working this summer. I need the money."

"You don't work that much," he says. "And the gas bar isn't even open Tuesdays. Why aren't you playing Men's League?"

I take a long drink from the bottle.

"I'm not good enough, Brian."

"So what? I mean, you'd never have made Blue, but you could always slap singles. And you're a good right fielder."

"A slap-hitting right fielder. Just what every team wants." I laugh. "A good right fielder is a bad ball-player. It's where you bury home run hitters, just to keep them in the line-up."

Now Brian takes a long pull on his beer. He used to pitch, but he shot up eight inches this school year. He can't hit the broadside of a barn with his throws now.

"I play right field."

"Yeah," I say, "and you hit home runs."

He laughs.

"Once in a while."

I get up and walk to the woodpile again, where I choose a big block for the fire. It kicks up a few sparks from the old coals, reignited from last night and the night before that. I stand and watch a moment, thinking, "It can be so peaceful out here," when Brian says, "Look up." Turning into the laneway is a boxy, maroon K-Car I recognize from Currie High School's student parking lot. Brian stands up when the engine quiets and he follows me around the side of the house. A door clatters shut as we turn the corner and meet Brian's older sister, Stella. She brushes wavy blond bangs from her eyes and adjusts an oversized white purse on her shoulder.

"What are you doing here?" Brian asks.

"Just out for a drive," she says. "With Jessie." She motions to the passenger side, where Jessie sits with one hand covering most of her face, her fingertips disappearing into her straight black hair. The bit of cheek we can see is pink, and the corner of a Ziploc bag of ice sticks out, squeezed in her fist.

"Shit," I say.

"Yeah," Stella says.

Brian walks to the car and taps the window, startling Jessie. She turns her head and bends toward the console, shielding her face.

"You O.K.?" Brian asks. "Come on out."

"Leave her alone," Stella says.

I look over my shoulder when I hear another vehicle accelerating toward the tracks. It's not Hank's pickup, like I expect, just another small sport truck with no muffler. It roars by.

"He's going to come looking for her," I say.

Stella smirks.

"At our house," she says, nodding at Brian. "But he'll never find us here."

"The car's on my front lawn! He'll fucking murder me!"

"So we'll move it," she says. "To the backyard. Close to the house."

"And leave wheel marks? No way! My parents—"

Stella laughs. "Your parents *might* kill you," she says "Hank *will*." She walks back to the car, not waiting for an answer, and she gets in and starts it. She reverses up the laneway then turns onto the lawn, rounding the house. She parks parallel to it, with the driver's side wheels nearly in Mom's flower beds, so close that after Jessie gets out the passenger side, still holding the ice to her eye, Stella has to follow, straddling the gearshift, worming her way over the seat and out the door.

Jessie takes a few steps away from the car, covering her face with both hands. She exhales and lets her hands fall to her sides. The pink was nothing compared to the purple that's darkening now below her eye. "Fuck it," she says, narrowing her eyes at me. "I know I look good with a shiner." I don't disagree. It suits her and her dingy red flip flops, toenails unpainted, bare legs under blue jean cut-offs and – no one's perfect – a faded black Doors T-shirt she's cut the neck out of. It sits off her shoulders and unabashedly shows a white bra strap. In her hand is a tiny red purse, barely bigger than the pack of cigarettes she pulls from it. She plucks one and puts it between her over-sticked lips, red, too. She lights up.

"Do you want to talk about it?" I ask.

"No," she says.

She bends over and opens the cooler. Bottles clink and ice rumbles. She stands up with her smoke pinched in her mouth, two beers in one hand as the other twists the caps, flicks them to the ground. She gives one bottle to Stella then lifts a hand to her mouth, lowering the cigarette to swig from the beer. Her hands come finally to rest at her sides again, bottle in one, cigarette the other. It is a good look for her.

er

Brian's watch alarm starts beeping. I'm soaked in sweat, and I didn't even sleep *in* the bag, just on it. We opened all the screens before passing out, but two guys and sixteen beers do this to a tent. It reeks. With my head pounding, I crawl to the door and unzip it, squirming out then walking barefoot on the grass toward the house. I open the screen door gently, tempering its squeal, remembering Jessie and Stella, who disappeared into the house after just one drink, and might still be asleep. But as I ease the door closed and enter through the laundry room I hear the shower running. I turn into the kitchen. Stella sits at the table flipping pages in a magazine.

"I got her a towel," she says. "A yellow one. From the hall closet. Is that O.K.?"

"It's fine."

She looks side to side, as though we're being watched.

"We'll go in a minute, once she's out."

"Go where?" I ask.

"Hank's leaving this morning for the lake, with the twins," Stella says. "We'll probably have breakfast at Don's to wait him out. Then I'll drop Jessie off."

"Hank's leaving her home alone?"

Stella rolls her eyes.

"It was going to be a trust exercise."

The judge had also ordered therapy.

"But it was him who hit her, right?" I ask.

Stella nods.

"Why?"

She shakes her head.

"You wouldn't believe me, and I can't tell you anyway." She fumbles in her purse for her car keys. "You guys want to come for breakfast?" she asks. "I'll drive you back after."

From the bathroom, the shower sound stops. In my mind I see Jessie take the towel from the rack. She dries her feet first and steps over the tub's edge now, wrapping the towel under her armpits, lifting out the wet hair that gets squeezed against her shoulders and letting it fall. Yellow's not her colour. She should take the towel off again.

"Mike?" Stella asks.

"Yeah," I say, back to reality. "Sounds good."

er

Don's Breakfast is full of farmers – *retired* farmers – like it is every Saturday. They've eaten here every weekend of their lives, and sat at the same tables every time, watching us young people, hangovers and all, as we get coffee before our shifts in the strip mall across the street at the Giant Tiger or Canada's Smallest Canadian Tire. When we sit down to fat and salt plates to flush the night before away, people whisper about our mismatched socks, (Brian), our messy hair, (me), or our wrinkled clothes, (Jessie, who slept in the T-shirt). Stella's the only one who looks half-decent, having packed before she drove out. We feel the stares as we walk to a booth at the back, though it could be worse: most times, we wait on display in the vestibule. About all Don can cook is a fried egg sandwich, but on Saturdays the line-up's out the door regardless.

Brian and I each get the Strapping Lad, three of everything: eggs, sausages, bacon and ham slices, and toast and home fries on the side. Stella gets the sandwich and Jessie gets nothing, just a coffee when the server says "And something to drink?" before she and her change pouch jingle off and leave our table in silence, the kind that would go unnoticed most hangover mornings. Sitting across from Jessie and her still-puffy eye, it looms like a funnel cloud. The coffee arrives, and then our plates. Jessie watches us devour our meals. I convince her to have a slice of my toast. She turns down the jam. When we finish our food Brian and I stare at Jessie. Stella stares at us. She pushes away her plate. The farmers are still staring at our table. Jessie glances at each of us in turn.

"Done?" she asks.

We look to each other, agreeing that we are, but before we answer Jessie has pushed herself up with her hands and brought her feet onto the bench. She stands and steps up onto the table and screams: "*I had an abortion, and my father hit me for it!*"

Forks clatter down on plates. Conversations end. Jessie jumps down from the table. She stalks to the front door and out. Stella and I each throw a twenty on the table, way more than the bill will come to. We forget the change and hurry after Jessie, finding her in Stella's passenger seat. We join her in the car and leave Currie, down the Tenth Concession toward Waubnakee.

When we're out of town, I lean forward and ask: "Who told him?"

Jessie sighs, doesn't look back. "Mitchell himself. After ball one night."

Dave Mitchell. Currie Blue's Number One Pitcher, and a star now in Men's League, the only league scouting out here. I didn't think he and Jessie were officially together, but I guess they are. Or were. I hope it's were.

Jessie turns and looks out her window. She exhales. "Hank and I were doing so well, too."

In the cluttered yard in front of the Muellers' leaning, mint-coloured house, we don't see the baby-blue truck. Stella pulls the car off just past the long laneway, to back in. She keeps it running. When Jessie gets out she leaves her door open. We wait in silence as she enters the house, holding our breath till she emerges again. She flashes a thumbs-up. No Hank, no speeding escape. No chase down gravel roads.

3

The men's team is in first place going into the playoffs. The final game is Labour Day Sunday, like always, but it's at night, pushed back by the girls' year-end tourney, which rotates between Currie and Somewhere Else every year. As the new team this year, Waubnakee is Somewhere Else.

The girls' last game of the season was their best, a 2-1 loss to Blue. The twins have played even better since Hank began coaching, as of the first game after the lake weekend. He yells a lot – "*Rebecca! Two hands!*" or "*Dammit, Stacey! Choke up!*" – but it's working. Most of the girls haven't improved, but a shortstop, a centre fielder and decent pitching can really carry a team: we finished a distant second, one win ahead of White.

I get to the diamond early, to unlock the equipment shed behind the backstop for Bob the Umpire, so he can spike the bases down. Hank's already on the field when I arrive, wearing his Wanderers jersey and leading the twins in furious jumping jacks. I sit in the bleachers and watch. Shawn's van pulls in and Christine and Samantha jump out the side door. They jog to the field. Shawn shakes his head as he approaches, rolled up bat rack in hand. His eyes dart side to side and he smiles.

"Hammerin' Hank." He shrugs. "What can you do?" He hands me the schedule the league office sent him and I walk it to the snack bar. I take the cover off the chalkboard beside the window and begin posting game times. To my left, a voice, not Jessie's, asks, "Can you give me a hand?" It's Jane Mueller, Jessie and the twins' mom, and she's been running the canteen for a month now. I hold up one corner of the flap as she undoes the padlock. We lower the plywood together.

"Thank you," she says, adjusting her glasses.

I say, "No problem." She lingers a moment, expecting small talk, I think, but I don't say more. I haven't seen Jessie since that morning at Don's, and I haven't asked – I wouldn't dare, not with Hammerin' Hank so close – but Brian told me, after Stella told him: Jessie's sentence is up.

er

Waubnakee plays first, against the team from the Reserve. I say it that way because everyone else calls them the Reds or the Indians, and the league has decked them out in knock-off Cleveland gear that's even more embarrassing than the mismatched ball pants and raglans their other teams wear, amassed second-hand. Only two adults accompany the team, one to coach and the other to drive their rusty mini school bus. Our girls take the field for the top of the first and I know that today, we'll do the mercying.

Mercying. Hank made it a verb in his speech before the game.

"Remember how it felt to get *mercied?*" he asked. He gestured to the three keeners from Blue in the bleachers, there early enough to see our game. "They know you're comin'," he said. "And we almost *beat* 'em last time." He paused for effect. "Run up the score. Send a message."

In the bottom of three, the girls walk off the field with the score 15-0 for us. No matter how bad you've got it, someone's always got it worse.

er

I'm watching our second game closely, from the coach's box at third base. We're up 7-5 in the fourth, runner on third, one out, when behind right field, the baby-blue pick-up pulls in; Hank's on the bench, though. The door opens and Jessie steps down, slamming it behind her. She walks toward the diamond in a fuchsia golf shirt. What's left of her hair has been cropped into a bob, more conservative but somehow more punk rock than even the old look, black eye notwithstanding. Watching her, I don't hear a deep foul ball ping, well over my head and still in play. White's left-fielder races toward the fence and crashes in, catching it. From the bench, Hank hollers, "Tag! Tag!"

The runner, Melissa, looks at me quizzically.

"Yes!" I yell. "Run! That means run!"

She pushes off and starts toward home, getting to the plate just before the throw, without sliding. Most of the girls are still scared to slide. On the back of my neck I feel Hank's glare burning, but I don't turn to look at the bench.

Jessie's just sat down in the bleachers.

She waves at me, ever so slightly.

et

In the top of the last inning, with two out, White scores two runs on a base-clearing double by a speedy red-head named Crystal, making the score 8-7. The next batter steps in and White's bench sings: *H-O, H-O-M, H-O-M-E-R-U-N, HOME RUN! SUZANNE!*, complete with handclaps. The batter, short with long brown hair, swings at the first pitch and scuffs it. The ball rolls slowly toward third base, barely past the pitcher. Rebecca charges hard and calls off Christine – "Mine! *Miine!*" – before scooping it and whipping it off-balance to first base, beating the runner by half a step and ending the game. Our girls run onto the field and celebrate around Melissa, who made the catch, throwing their gloves in the air and cheering. They're through to the final. As they line up at the plate for the handshake, a hand shoves my shoulder from behind and I stumble. I turn around. Hank stands with his arms folded, nostrils flaring.

"Get your head in the game, *Carrion*," he says, poking my chest. "Your old boy would be so disappointed. We nearly didn't score that. What the hell were you thinking?"

"I don't know," I say. "I'm sorry."

He takes off his cap, revealing a balding skull. "These girls have to *win*," he says. He wipes his forehead with the back of his hand. "You understand?"

I nod.

"What?" he barks.

"Yes," I say, straightening my spine and lifting my head, which is finally enough for him. He replaces his hat and stalks off toward Shawn. They talk in low tones then head for Shawn's van. I walk to the bleachers. Around us, Blue's players are rising from their seats, gathering their equipment. One starts walking toward the diamond, around the backstop to her bench on the third-base line. Jessie and I sit in silence as Blue takes the field, one girl batting grounders to a few teammates on the base paths. Our players have begun walking toward the parking lot, where they'll get into parents' vehicles and ride to Shawn's place for barbecued hamburgers before the final. Passing them the other way is the Reserve team, leaving the rusty team bus for their last meaningless game. Jessie watches absently as they sleepwalk toward the diamond. She exhales heavily.

"What?" I ask.

She turns to me, then looks away again.

"No," she says. "It's too corny."

"Come on. What?" I ask again.

"Well," she starts, "it's just... this has been really good for Rebecca and Stacey... and for the other girls, too. I mean, something to throw themselves into, and..."

"And what?"

"And it makes me wonder if things could have been different for me."

She leans forward to pick a few blades of grass and tosses them up, letting the breeze take them.

"Hank always wanted me to play, too," she says. "On the boys' team."

I imagine her sliding in a dust cloud at second base – cleats up, of course – with a black stripe under each eye. She stands and dusts herself off, looking back at first base, nodding her approval. (I moved her over, hustling out the bunt.)

She's waiting for me to say something.

"Would you have liked that?" I ask.

She looks in my eyes for an extra long moment.

"No," she says. She looks away. "No. I fucking hate softball."

I reach over and take her hand. She doesn't pull away but she says, "Not here." She lets go and rises from her seat. I stand and follow her along the first-base fence, to Hank's pickup. My pickup. Jessie takes a crowded ring of keys from her purse. She puts one in my door.

"He left you the truck?"

"His ball equipment, too," she says, smiling, unlocking it.

"Trust exercise?"

"It is now," she says.

I pull my door shut as she gets behind the wheel. She starts the engine and reaches for Hank's Rothmans on the dashboard, putting one in her mouth and offering me the pack. I don't smoke but I take one, which she lights for me. I breathe in and cough. She cracks the window and shifts the truck into drive. We turn off the park laneway at the museum, onto Waubnakee's one back street, and then we accelerate onto County Road 17. We vault the tracks in front of my house. Jessie keeps the pedal depressed. My knuckles go white around the armrest on the door.

"Relax," she says. "I have my licence."

Same grade but older, I remember.

"Where are we going?" I ask. She doesn't answer or even glance away from the windshield.

"What happened to you, Jessie? Where've you been?"

She takes the last drag on her cigarette and throws it out the window. She finally takes her eyes off the road.

"Don't laugh," she says.

"I won't."

"Bible Camp," she says. I keep my promise and let Jessie break first. Her laugh is loud, too loud, and it scares me. It sounds hungry. "The day after I saw you, when my parents came home... they drove me to Bible Camp. Four weeks. I got back yesterday."

"And Mitchell?" I ask.

She turns to me again, eyes wide, mad.

"What about him?"

"Did you two talk about—"

"No," she says. "Not really. He's going to college. He thinks he broke up with me, but..."

"But?"

"We haven't talked," she says. "Not since I told him about" – she pauses – "*the baby.*"

We near the dirt road along the Waubnakee River – River Road – and turn onto it. We follow it until it can't help but cross. Jessie stops the truck on the clattering steel bridge, so close to the barrier that she nearly scrapes it, trapping me inside the cab. If I want out, I'll have to go through her, but she leads, opening her door and jumping down. I hear the tailgate clang and the truck's old springs groan, her footsteps echoing in the chassis. I open the back window to talk to her, but when I see her I know she won't answer. She stops and stares down at Hank's equipment bag. A frog croaks. Jessie bends suddenly – violently – and she lifts the bag by its straps, swaying with it a moment before she screams, low and throaty, "*I hate you!*" and throws it over the railing. She loses her balance and thuds on the truck floor. The bats and balls clunk on the rocks. The river's nearly dry this late in summer.

"He's going to kill you," I say.

Jessie shakes her head.

"Everyone knows, now," she says. She sniffs. "All he can do is send me away."

She lifts one foot over the side of the box, and using the tire as a foothold she jumps down.

"Is that what you want?" I ask. But as though she doesn't hear, Jessie walks to her still-open door. She lifts off her shirt and throws it in at me. She steps up from the running board. She lunges at my fly.

er

Jessie lets me out at the end of the park lane, on her way home to pack what she can. A few Waubnakee players' cars are already in the parking lot, so we don't kiss goodbye. I make up something to tell Shawn about scouting Blue's pitcher, but when I get to the bench he doesn't ask.

After warm up, Hank herds the girls into the cage. He stands in the doorway and talks of trophies and execution. Shawn and I flank him and add nothing.

"And last thing," Hank says. "Nobody – I mean *nobody* – swings at the first pitch. If you do, you sit the next inning. It's about discipline. Make her throw you strikes."

Blue's the top seed, so they're the home team. Their pitcher comes out tired in the top of the first – starting her third game today – and she throws us twelve straight balls and loads the bases. Rebecca steps in next and clears them with a double – second pitch, a fast one, way outside. She calls, "Come on, Stace," as her sister takes a bat and walks to the plate. The first pitch to Stacey comes in slower than it should, straight down the pipe, and she swings and powers the ball over the outfielders. It booms off the black tile atop the fence, inches from where Hank usually puts it, and the ball caroms back past the centre fielder, who gives chase in vain. The easy home run makes the score 5-0. It's Stacey's first homer, and if the plaque-'n'-shack would just make some room, it would be the league distance record, too. At the plate, Rebecca waits and slaps her sister high-ten when she crosses. The grinning twins return to the bench, where the team has lined up to greet them. Hank waits behind the fence and glares. Stacey meets his eyes. Her smile disintegrates. She slumps and drags her feet as she walks off the field, arms lowered, ignoring the high-fives. The girls stand aside and let Stacey shuffle down the bench in silence. The whole team turns and stares at scowling Hank, who ignores them and looks at his clipboard. He calls the next name: Nancy. She walks to the plate.

We've made Nancy bunt a lot this season – it's the only way to get her on base. She looks at me and waits for the sign, but I don't tap my belt buckle or dust off my arms. We exchange a glance.

Fuck him. Swing away.

The first pitch is good and Nancy rips past it wildly. She cuts again at the second, a mile outside. She connects on the third, in on her wrists, and she pops up lamely to the catcher. As usual, the bench greets her with half-hearted "Good try" and "You'll get her next time," which we taught the girls to say after a tough out, when really there's nothing to say at all. Nancy takes her seat at the end of the bench, beside Stacey.

Melissa hits next, and she doesn't even look at me. She swings through three straight, and so does Samantha. Blue hustles off. Six of our girls retrieve their gloves and take the field. Four others stay glued to the bench.

Melissa's green eyes gleam.

"You can't sit us all," she taunts Hank.

Bob the Umpire calls, "Hurry up, Yellow!" Hank grunts and sends everyone but Stacey out, opting to play one short just to make his point, and, in his haste, he sends Nancy to centre field. As if they're aiming at her – which they well might be – Blue's players pound ball after ball over her head. Eight runs come in, the limit for the inning, and after Waubnakee goes down in order in the top of the second – three more swinging strikeouts – Blue scores the maximum again. We get nothing in the top of three: long fly out for Rebecca, strikeout for Stacey, and a pop-up to the pitcher by Nancy. Blue scores a quick four runs in the bottom.

20-5.

Bob waves a hand at Hank.

"Mercy rule," he announces. "Game's over."

Blue cheers and rushes from their bench. Hank leaps off ours and kicks the bat rack off the fence. He throws everything he can find on the field: batting helmets, spare gloves, the scorebook, more, and he storms toward the parking lot. Shawn and I line our girls up for the handshake. Blue gets the trophy and, afterward, the Waubnakee parents greet their daughters in the bleachers, where they put hands on shoulders and sigh and walk together to their cars.

Nancy helps me retrieve the team gear from the field, and at the shed we meet Shawn, unlocking it for Bob, who takes a hammer and walks back to the diamond. We wait while he moves the bases back, for the Men's final.

Shawn asks Nancy, "Think you'll be back next year?"

Nancy stares through him. She doesn't answer.

"It's alright," he says. "I'm not sure either."

Nancy and I say goodbye to Shawn and we follow the third-base line out of the park. We turn down the back street. We cross the tracks. From our lawn, we can still hear Hank, cursing in the parking lot. I picture the twins and Jane in the van, rigid in their seats, making sure to not look out the door at him. He calls Jessie's name, over and over, and I wonder how far she'll get this time.

Amy Stuart

THE ROUNDNESS

I count eleven people waiting at the gate. Eight men in suits, a lady with a baby, and me. That's eleven, if you count the baby.

My aunt said, Wait a week before flying. Wait for your mother to come get you. I said, I want to go home for Christmas. My aunt cried all the way to the airport. The snow was only starting, those flakes on the windshield and for that split second you see them, all tiny, before they melt against the glass.

At the gate, I find the seat next to the window. All I've got is my backpack. The maternity clothes are in a garbage bag in my aunt's basement, back to Goodwill they go. I press my face against the glass. The guys in the orange vests stand around the tarmac with their faces tucked in. One of them is wearing goggles, like some old-time pilot, goggles and a hat with ear flaps. I wave but he doesn't see me.

Our plane pulls up. Next to the jetliners it looks like a toy, one of those twin engines with propellers and nine windows on each side. Who wants to fly to Hearst? What if there's no bathroom? I still pee every ten minutes and the pee is still pink. Sometimes chunks come out with it. The nurse said, You'll need the diapers for the bleeding. She called them absorbent underwear. The doctor said, Expect clots. Anything smaller than a deck of cards is okay. Anything bigger isn't.

Airports are full of glass. Everywhere I look, there I am. I'm walking like an old lady and I'm fat. Fat like I'm still pregnant. The roundness has shrunk but it's still there, hanging off my front. The doctor said, It'll take a month for the uterus to reduce back to normal, the size of a fist. I clenched and said, Whose fist? Yours or mine?

Before we board I call my mom. She's crying too. At the gate the pilots show up, two men with good posture, navy suits with golden cuffs. The way they laugh and chit chat with the flight attendant, no one seems too worried about the snow. So what if the clouds swallow us up? They have gauges and dials for that.

The lady with the baby gets up and walks him. Him because everything around her is blue. I see the tiniest hand poke out from the blanket, open and shut in a wave, grasping at the air. When he starts to cry the cramps roll through my gut and I breathe in, breathe out. There's a hot tickle in my chest. The nurse said, In a day or two, the milk will come.

———

Nancy noticed first. We worked at Baskin Robbins and by the end of summer I was round all over. She'd bulge her eyes out at me. Stand back! she'd say. That uniform can barely contain your jugs! I'm getting fat, I said to my mom. Too much ice cream. I shook my jugs in her face. Look at these! That's when she clued in. She went to the drugstore and I peed on the stick and sure enough. We went to the doctor and he stuck me with the ultrasound wand and the baby's all perfect with its fingers and toes, eyes, ears, mouth and nose. Curled up as big as a head of lettuce. The doctor said, You're five months along.

Jesus, my mom said, all calm in her way. Look what you've done.

On the drive home she said nothing so I told her. It was only once. At a party, Good Friday if you can believe it, a boy named Patrick, a twelfth grader. We were on the top bunk and Nancy and her boy on the bottom, and Patrick pushed my pants to my ankles. He said, Can we do it? and I said nothing, so there you have it. My mom said, A twelfth grader? That boy should be shot.

———

It's seven o'clock when we board the plane. The eleven of us across the tarmac, huddled and shuffling like penguins. The lady with the baby sits across the aisle from me. All the other rows are taken, I have no choice. The mess of blue blankets is quiet now, and once we're in our seats the mother looks at me and smiles and I think, she could never guess. Even with the shrinking roundness still tucked under my sweatshirt, she would never guess.

———————

When we got home from the ultrasound I taped the picture into my journal. A white blob floating in a black circle, a baby. Lying on my bed with my shirt pulled up, it seemed so obvious, I wondered how I could have missed it. Nancy's sister had a baby in the spring. She got so huge they had to cut off her wedding ring at the jewellery store. Then her baby came out so fat its eyes were puffed shut and Nancy said it looked Asian. My mom said, That's racist. It's racist to look Asian? I said.

After a while my mom came into my room and sat next to me on the bed and said, You'll give it up. Move to Toronto and live with Auntie Kate. Like they used to do before abortion and the pill. I told her what Nancy told me once. In the States they still abort babies until eight months and if it comes out alive the doctor stabs it with a scalpel. My mom slapped me across the face. Then she buried her face in her hands.

You're only fourteen, she said.

I said, It's okay. I'll go.

———

The flight attendant shows us how to put on the oxygen mask and life jackets. She says to the mother, When the plane takes off hold the baby on your shoulder, like you're burping him. Hold on tight. We taxi away from the airport and out into the black and whiteness, the only lights on the ground, green and flickering. A gust of wind and the plane shudders. One of the men in suits says, Anyone need life insurance? I can sell you some before we take off! Everyone laughs, even the flight attendant. Everyone except for me and the mother.

———

We got to Toronto at the end of August. My aunt lives in the smallest house pushed right up against the sidewalk, all the downtown buildings out her living room window. She left Hearst and never came back. There's this alternative school by my office, my aunt said, only a couple dozen students, hippie dippy teachers. No one there'll bat an eye at you.

When my mom had to leave there were big tears, her face all wet and snotty. I'll quit my job, she said. Nonsense, my aunt said. They're identical twins. Sometimes they hug pressed so tightly together that they look Siamese, two-headed. At the bus station they squeezed me between them and the roundness flipped and flopped and my mom pulled back and looked down at my belly wide-eyed, she felt it too. By the look on her face I wondered if she was going to pull the chute. As in, Let's keep it. A grandma at thirty-eight. But instead she kissed my forehead and nodded to her sister the doppelganger, and then she was gone, gobbled up by the revolving doors.

The propellers are quiet. Over the intercom the pilot says, Sorry about the delay folks. More snow than we expected! The flight attendant comes by with bags of candied nuts. The mother says, How long will we be? The flight attendant shrugs. Who can tell with snow? In my backpack I have a sandwich and yogurt and an ice pack to keep them cold. If you need to you can sit on it, my aunt said. The ice pack, she meant. If I needed to, I could sit on the ice pack.

They call it relinquishment.

The high school had a social worker and I had weekly meetings. She had a binder full of questions. Her office smelled like coffee. Do I smoke? Did I drink? Well, I said, there was that twenty-sixer of rum behind the Baskin Robbins with Nancy and her boy. Were you pregnant then? When was that? I thought of it in terms of coats. If it was cold, if I was wearing a coat, I wasn't pregnant yet. Behind the Baskin Robbins we could see our breath in steamy cones as we huddled and took swigs. So, no. I wasn't pregnant.

The social worker wanted me to look at profiles. Couples who want babies. At Thanksgiving my mom flew to Toronto and we looked through binders together at my aunt's kitchen table. Pictures of husbands and wives lying on grass with their dogs. Lawyers and teachers. Actors and writers. Unable to conceive. These two look really nice, my mom said. My aunt said, These people depress me. My mom stood up and marched out of the kitchen. She plopped herself on the living room couch and hollered at us, Just because you don't want it doesn't mean it's not worth having!

Some good it did you! my aunt hollered back. Your husband's long gone, isn't he?

When the baby cries again, something bursts. Two wet circles on my sweatshirt, expanding out. I cross my arms and press into the hardness. The milk is warm and I am throbbing. The mother paces the aisle and now she is crying too, and I want the propellers to roar and drown it all out, but we aren't moving, no one is moving, all this stillness, and out the window more snow, piling up on the sill.

Do something, the mother says to the flight attendant. Can't you do something?

The pilot's voice says, No gates, folks. We may be here a while yet!

The mother sits down and sticks the bottle into the baby's mouth but the bottle is still empty and when the mother throws it hard to the ground it rolls under the seat and then rocks back against her foot, back and forth.

———————

We picked the couple with the fluffy dog. A closed adoption, everyone agreed. There will be a time for babies. Maybe in a decade or two, my aunt said. In the bathroom one Wednesday afternoon, a glob in my underwear and then the cramps. They said forty weeks, this was thirty-seven. The roundness like a heavy ball tipping me over. A gush of sticky water down my thighs. In an hour all the familiar faces at the hospital.

Your mother, said my aunt. I can't get a hold of her.

The nurse gave me ice water.

The adoptive parents are here, the social worker told us. In the waiting room.

No time for the needle, said the doctor. You are dilating too fast.

Gas her, someone said.

A mask on my face. I breathed in and the room faded until I was in the woods behind our old house in Hearst, where the ground used to crunch beneath my running shoes, and it must be cold because even the

147

leaves on the saplings have turned orange. The room came back and the nurse was wiping my forehead.

It is time, she said. Time to push.

The baby wails now, the airplane fills with it. The mother clutches him in the aisle, frantic. She says, You can't just leave us here all night! She screams, He'll starve!

When she passes I touch her arm.

I have milk, I say.

She blinks at me. I show her my wet sweatshirt.

I have milk for your baby.

She shakes her head.

Please, I say. Please?

Then the mother is beside me and we both fumble. She holds a blanket up. The baby is wrinkled and pink. He shakes his head wildly and she pries his mouth open and pushes him into me. With a jolt of pain his jaw starts clicking and I look at the mother. Success. She must feel the roundness and she must understand. If she wanted to she might say, You are too young. Or maybe, Look what you gave up. Instead she says, My milk wasn't enough. I never had enough. Well, I say, if you want he can have all of mine.

The little one is quiet and his mother strokes his head and everyone else on the plane is quiet too, and the flight attendant stands by the cockpit chewing on her fingernails, like this is everybody's business, a baby and his milk.

————

My aunt said, Look at her! You made her!

This crumple of gooey skin, eyes clamped shut and fists in angry balls. One of the nurses wrapped her up and walked out and the door clicked behind them but I could still hear her, crying in these jabs down the hall-way. Then the room was quiet except for the shuffle of the nurses and my aunt, my aunt with her sniffling smile. Brave girl, she said. My brave girl.

All the blood everywhere. Like a massacre. In the movies the baby slips out, just like that. No one tells you. My mom said, It will hurt. No one tells you. You are split open. The blood and guts that come after. It's like a whole other birth, the afterbirth. After they took her away the doctor told me to push again and he yanked on the umbilical cord and with a hiss out it came, fleshy and purple. The doctor said, Look at this. The placenta is an organ, a disposable heart. No one tells you. The doctor spun it on his fist like pizza dough, looking for holes.

The doctor said, The placenta is intact.

He threw it in a steel bowl and the nurse wheeled it away too.

When I woke up my aunt was asleep in the chair beside me. Papers to sign. I said, I feel okay. They gave me pills for the pain and diapers for the bleeding. More pills to slow the milk, but the nurse said, Nothing stops it outright. In a day or two, it will come.

———————

The baby knows just what to do but it still hurts. As the milk drains, everything tingles. The mother dabs at my cheeks with the blue blanket.

The propellers start and the little one drops off me, asleep, his mouth wide open and dribbling with milk. The mother lifts him onto her shoulder and then she lays a blanket over me. She says, Try to rest.

Out the window there is some blackness. The plane is moving. It might even be morning soon. The pilot says, Sorry about that, folks! My mom will be waiting for me at the airport, and my bed at home will be warm. My mom said, I put up the Christmas tree for you. When my eyes close I see her wrapped in a pink blanket and I think, They probably love her already, because they waited so long for her to come.

Phil Della

I DID IT
FOR YOU

For the last six months Bill has been going through the garbage in the staff lunchroom looking for pop cans to return for the deposit. Not wanting to be seen by anyone, he spends only a few seconds picking through the orange peels and coffee grounds at the top of the stinking bin for the easy cans. It pains him to abandon the cans that are deeper down, but he has his reputation to protect.

At his wife's work he goes through the garbage too. The trash there is a gold mine – his wife works at a college. Five minutes in these garbage cans is the equivalent of an hour out on the street scrounging.

"Bill!" his wife whispers from her office doorway. "What if someone sees you?"

Bill works quickly, with nervous glances over his shoulder, even though there are few people around at this time of the evening. All it takes is one person to notice him stooped over a hallway trash can.

"I have to work here," his wife reminds him quietly.

"I'm almost done," he reassures her.

"No more!" she insists.

Bill stands up straight, his cardboard box of cans cradled in his arms. "There, finished," he says.

∽⚬

While driving, Bill keeps his eyes on the edge of the roadway in search of cans. Once, he pulled over on a busy highway to pick up a string of cans, but only once. Now he leaves them behind for his fellow collectors who are less timid than he. On slower streets he often stops. If possible, he positions the car close beside a can for a discrete pick-up. In the unfortunate event that there are onlookers, he will almost always hold off for a better opportunity tomorrow, the next day, whenever he can schedule another drive-by.

Every day at home Bill washes his catch in the kitchen sink. With the coming of winter, some of the cans are now full of ice and take much rinsing with hot water. Most still hold the dregs of whatever was in them. The pop cans are sticky, the beer cans and bottles stink of hops and yeast. As Bill rinses them, cigarette butts emerge and settle in the drain of the stainless steel sink. One time, he forgot to clean the drain afterwards and his wife discovered the remains of a mouse. After that she told him to clean his junk outside.

On weekends, after long walks to collect cans, Bill redeems his catch at the store for the deposit. His wife hates to admit it, but the collecting of cans was sort of her idea. She had threatened that if Bill was foolish enough to get a speeding ticket he would have to pay it off by collecting cans. Bill has yet to get a ticket, but he likes her idea of punishment.

❧

Early Saturday morning Bill dresses for his weekend walk in warm but grubby clothing, since he knows he might get dirty. He sits on the floor of the entrance hall tying his boots, an old coat zipped up to his chin, a mismatched toque pulled down over his ears. Beside him lay two plastic shopping bags and a pair of ski gloves.

"Where are you going?" his wife inquires from the top of the stairs. She stands looking down at him in her knee-length robe, having just come out of the shower. She already knows where he is going. She wants to know if he knows where he is going, and he's not to be going anywhere. His wife wants them to spend the weekend together, like they used to, before the cans.

"I'm just going for a walk," he answers. "You want to come?"

His wife cannot get over how much her husband resembles a bum, dressed the way he is. A bum has replaced my husband, she's convinced.

"Where's my husband?" she calls down the stairs. "I want to talk with my husband."

"Are you coming or not?" he asks, taking off his toque.

He isn't really interested in her coming along. She's not any fun on an outing like this, he knows.

"You're not taking him out can-collecting are you?" she asks, trying her best to hide the anger with sweetness.

Bill doesn't answer because he thinks it's obvious.

"I wanted to spend a nice weekend with him," she pouts.

"I am coming back," he says.

"You're not my husband. You're the bum who's kidnapped him," she says.

"Is something the matter?" Bill asks.

His wife turns from the stairs on her way back to their bedroom. She drops the wet towel from her head onto the carpet and goes to the bathroom mirror with a hair pick to work out the tangles. She winces at the knots then impatiently pulls through them. Bill reluctantly comes up the stairs to deal with her.

"What's the matter this time?" he wants to know.

She is not interested in his insincere effort to work things out, and her hair is making matters worse. Bill has come into the bathroom now. He is trying to keep calm.

She avoids his eyes by looking down at the ends of her hair.

"What did I do?" he asks sincerely this time.

"You care more about your stupid cans than you do me," she tells him. "Every moment it's cans. You think I'm kidding, but you're not far from being a bum."

"I wish I were a bum," Bill replies. "Then I wouldn't care what anybody thought. I could rummage for cans and screw anybody looking."

"You may care what others think, but you don't care what I think," she counters. "I'm less in your eyes than a total stranger."

Bill does not reply; his words have lost their persuading power. His wife throws her comb down on the counter and storms out, slamming the door to their bedroom. Bill knows this weekend will be a write-off as far as cans are concerned.

∞⋉∞

On his way to work Monday morning, Bill turns down a few back roads in search of cans – in an attempt to make up for his wasted weekend. He spends more time than he should and gets nothing to show for it. Arriving at the office late, he discovers two empty pop cans on his desk. He wonders who put them there and why. Does someone know I go through the garbage, he wonders? He leaves them where they are until he works up the nerve to say something.

"Who left their crap on my desk?" he says aloud to no one in particular.

When no one responds, he picks up the pop cans and makes a big deal about throwing them away.

"Why can't people throw their own crap into the garbage?" he says.

"Those were for you," says the receptionist with a smile. She is a young, new employee.

Bill doesn't know how to respond. Everyone is listening he thinks.

"I thought you recycled them," she says.

"At home I do," he agrees. "It's better than throwing them away."

He picks them up out of the garbage and walks into the lunchroom for his morning coffee. He wants to end the discussion about himself and cans before too much is revealed. While he is stirring the cream and sugar into his cup, the receptionist hurries in. From the lunchroom it is difficult to answer the phone in time, so she cannot stay long. The young girl comes right up to him grabbing his arm.

"I have more cans at my place," she says. "I'll bring them for you tomorrow."

Pulling his arm free of her grip, Bill wants to tell her to forget about the cans – to shut up about them –

especially when others are around. But he secretly wants her cans very badly.

"How many do you have?" he asks.

"I don't know," she rolls her eyes. "I never counted them, but I have lots."

"Ten?" Bill ventures.

"More like hundreds," she tells him.

Bill cannot believe his good fortune. Still, what if it gets out he's accepting cans from his co-worker? It might look bad.

"You should take them in yourself," he tells her.

She shakes her head as the phone rings in the distance. "I can't be bothered with that," she says.

"No," insists Bill. "I shouldn't take them."

"I'll bring some for you tomorrow," she insists, on her way out the door.

"No!" Bill practically shouts. He doesn't want them at work. "Don't bring them here. I'll come for them myself."

The receptionist agrees immediately. "How about tonight? Can you come tonight?"

Bill nods in silence. Tonight it is.

⁘

Bill arrives home before his wife, which is unusual since she works much closer to home. In an effort to make up for a strained weekend, Bill decides to prepare dinner. Not the regular cook, he stumbles around the kitchen looking for the ingredients to tacos, his favourite meal. He takes some hamburger out of the freezer and starts it cooking in the frying pan. All the while he's wondering how to get away for the cans.

When his wife opens the front door, Bill runs over to shout down the stairs. "I'm making dinner. How was your day, honey?"

His wife slowly ascends with her arms weighed down by two heavy grocery bags. "There's more in the car," she says, dropping the two bags onto the carpet at the top of the stairs.

"You went shopping," he notices. He remembers he should be stirring the meat on the stove and hurries away. "How was shopping?" he says over his shoulder.

His wife is too tired to talk about it, and there are tons of groceries in the car that it now appears she will have to lug upstairs by herself. She decides they can wait and walks over behind her husband to see what's frying in the pan. While Bill stirs the meat she remembers what happened at work today.

"Guess what Brian Moore told me?" she begins.

"Who's he?" Bill asks.

"I work with him," she says. "I see him every day."

Bill can detect an edge of annoyance in her voice. He turns the heat down on the element so the meat won't burn.

"He saw you walking," she explains. "He asked me if we had moved."

"Moved?" Bill repeats puzzled. "We haven't moved." Bill stops stirring the meat to listen more carefully.

"He said he wondered why you were so far away from home carrying two grocery bags. He wanted to know what you were doing."

It dawns on Bill what his wife is getting at. She's talking about the cans.

"What did you tell him?" he asks nervously.

"I said you were a weirdo who goes out looking for cans in ditches."

"You didn't!" Bill bursts out.

His wife laughs. She has him right where she wants him.

"Who is this guy again?" Bill asks.

His wife explains until it is clear to Bill exactly who he is.

"I've invited Brian and his wife over for dinner tomorrow," she says, looking with anticipation for his reaction.

"This is ready," says Bill. "Let's eat."

"I can understand why you wouldn't want to have them over," his wife goes on. "I'm sure he'll ask what you were doing."

Bill is putting the plates onto the table. He reaches down the cups and pulls out some napkins.

His wife watches him from the sink where she is squeezing all the water she possibly can out of the dishrag before cleaning the mess Bill has made of the stove.

"I have to go out after dinner," he says as he sits down to eat.

"What for?" his wife asks.

"It's a little errand," he says. "Work-related."

His wife is annoyed. She doesn't like how his work treats him.

"Don't they get enough out of you in eight hours?" she starts. She has an entire sermon on the mistreatment her husband suffers at the hand of his boss.

"It's no big deal," says Bill, before crunching into his taco. It only takes one bite but half the taco falls apart all over his plate.

⟡

Without calling ahead to say he's coming, Bill sets out in his car for the cans. It's a bit of a drive, and every minute it takes makes Bill less at ease. The receptionist lives in an apartment, the first place of her very own. Bill buzzes her from the main entrance and waits to be let in. He waits for a minute and gets no reply. Great, he thinks. All this way for diddly squat. He scolds himself for not calling ahead. This is the biggest waste of time, he tells himself. He decides to leave, then buzzes one more time just in case. Another minute elapses and he turns to go.

"Hello," comes her voice. "I was in the shower."

Bill runs back to the speaker but hesitates. My wife is not going to like this, he thinks. Is this really worth it? I can still back out now.

"I'm sorry I took so long," says her voice. "Come on up." The lock to the front door releases without Bill saying a word. He pulls the door open and makes his way up. I did come all this way, he thinks. I might as well. As he walks down the hall toward her door, he sees her standing at the threshold in her robe drinking a can of something.

"Come on in," she says. "Do you want one?" she asks, holding up a can of pop.

"I can't stay long," he explains, shaking his head.

She closes the door behind him as he surveys the apartment. It's a wreck of cans everywhere. As he passes her she latches onto his arm.

"I'm so glad you came," she says.

"You must have had a wild party," he observes.

"It was awesome," the receptionist tells him. "I'm sorry I didn't invite you."

"I probably wouldn't have fit in," he says.

"Oh, no! We had some older guys here too," she says. "I like older guys, you know. They're more mature."

"Some of them," says Bill, finally able to wrench his arm free of her grip.

"I can give you the tour now," the receptionist announces, hooking his arm with hers again. She starts with the steamy bathroom, then the kitchen – with its bright orange counter top from the 1970s – and finally the couchless living room furnished with only two plastic patio chairs and a 12-inch television placed on a TV tray. But there are lots of cans and bottles.

"I guess I should get started," he suggests.

The receptionist disappears into her bedroom, leaving Bill to his cans. In the living room he shakes open a large, black garbage bag and hustles around after the cans. If he were outside he would dump the dregs onto the ground, but here it takes him longer making trips to the sink. Before long the receptionist returns wearing a sleeveless, red dress, which ends above her knees. She removes a beer from the refrigerator, pops the tab and sets it down by the sink in front of Bill.

"Don't be shy," she says.

To be polite, Bill has a sip. All he thinks is that it means one more can for him. He sets the beer down and picks up an empty to shake out over the sink. The receptionist does the same and they make their way more quickly down the kitchen counter to the dining area and down the hall to the bathroom. The receptionist empties two bottles of beer into the toilet while Bill stoops over the tub to reach a can by the back tile. When he grabs the can the receptionist pulls the shower handle. Before Bill can back away, his hair and shirt are soaked and dripping with warm water. The receptionist giggles as she flees.

"I couldn't help myself," she says between gasps of breath.

Bill dries his hair off with her towel.

"Don't get any more ideas," he says.

Bill gets down to business in the living room; he throws the cans into his bag whether they are empty or not; he will deal with the mess later. The receptionist, however, is in no hurry. She carries one can at a time to the kitchen sink and even rinses it out with water. Eventually the only room left is her bedroom. Bill checks his watch and checks it again. It's later than he thought. He wants to get out of here before it's too late. The receptionist enters her bedroom and opens the window. She shakes a can out the window, dumping the contents onto a bush below.

"Hey," she calls. "There's more for you in here."

Bill does not go into her room. He looks at his watch one more time. Finally the receptionist comes out to get him.

"You'll like what's in here," she says, pulling his arm.

Bill can finally see what's inside. It is clear she has been saving these up for a long time. The whole wall behind her bed is stacked to the ceiling with cans. Bill walks up to them in amazement. The receptionist jumps onto her bed, reaches for a can and hands it to Bill.

"I've been building it ever since I was a little girl. If you look you'll notice every can is different. I thought they would fit into my new apartment, but they make it look too much like a little girl's room. I want you to have them."

"No." Bill refuses. "It's not right for me to take this. You should save it."

"I'm sick of saving cans," she says.

"This is special," he says. "You can't go giving this to just anybody."

"I'm not. I want you to have them. You appreciate cans more than anyone I know. I want you to have mine."

Bill considers for a moment but all he can think to say is, "No."

"Why not?" demands the receptionist. "You're taking all the other ones. What's the difference?"

"I don't know," admits Bill. "But you should keep these."

"You're weird. You sound like my dad," she says. "He didn't even want me to take them out of the house. I'm not a little girl anymore. I can do whatever I want with my cans."

Bill can tell it's time to leave. He goes into the kitchen to wash his hands, but when he turns to say goodbye he finds the door to her bedroom shut. Bill wants to go but not without saying goodbye. Finally he knocks on the door.

"See you at work," he says through the door.

The receptionist comes out past him; this time she is dressed in pajamas. She goes into the kitchen and comes back with his beer.

"You never finished your beer," she says in an annoyed tone. "I should have known you were a waster."

"I have to get home," he explains. "My wife is expecting me."

"I'd like to meet this wife of yours," she says.

Bill opens the front door and steps out to leave. "I'll see you at work," he says.

He waves goodbye as the receptionist watches him leave. When he gets out to his car he can hear the receptionist yelling his name. She's standing in her bedroom window holding up the bag of cans.

"You forgot your cans!" she yells.

"No I didn't!" Bill yells back. He opens his car door, gets in and is away.

❧

Parking the car on the street at home, Bill notices all the lights in the house are out except their bedroom light. He opens the front door and takes off his shoes before running up the stairs and into their bedroom. His wife is sitting on the edge of the bed in her pajamas with the phone receiver in hand.

"I almost called the police," she tells him for shock value.

"Sorry I'm late. It took longer than I expected," is Bill's reply.

"What on earth were you doing anyway?" she wants to know.

He wonders if he should tell her. All he can think to say is, "Cans."

"Cans!" shouts his wife. "This was all for cans? What am I going to do with you? No more cans. I can't take it any more."

"You don't understand," he tries to explain.

"You said it was for work," she reminds him.

"The receptionist at work, they were her cans."

"You have no business going after someone else's cans. It's... it's... whose cans were they?"

"The receptionist's."

"Which one's she?"

"The one that answers the phone."

"The grabby one?"

"She's a grabber all right."

His wife grabs him by the arm. "Oh, Bill, you have such big muscles."

"She wants to meet you," Bill tells her.

"I'd like to see this one," says his wife.

"She's so grabby. She was grabbing me the whole time I was there."

His wife examines her husband's face.

"Quit smirking. You liked it."

"No. Seriously," he reassures her.

"You like her. Went to collect her cans. Why couldn't she bring them to work?"

"I don't want everybody at work to know about the cans."

"Maybe I should tell them what you really are up to," his wife threatens.

"Anyway," says Bill. "You'll be happy to know I left the cans there."

His wife is unimpressed, shaking her head.

"I just walked away. I said 'no.'"

"You spent the whole evening over there with her and now you have to go back tomorrow night," she reinterprets.

"No! You should be proud of me. I'm through with cans. I don't want to see another can."

"Why don't I believe you?" says his wife.

"And there were lots of cans. She had a whole wall of them, and they could have been mine. And do you know why I didn't take them? It's because of you. I did it for you, because I really wanted her cans. I wish I had them. But I resisted."

His wife pulls back the covers on her side of the bed. She checks the clock to see if the alarm is set, then flicks off the light.

"What's the matter now?" Bill says in bewilderment.

"Why don't you just go and get her cans. You obviously want them."

Bill flicks on the light.

"I thought you would be happy," he says, kneeling beside the bed. But his wife keeps her eyes closed. "I did it for you," he says.

His wife's face comes to life. "You did it for me," she says. "And that's supposed to make me feel better?"

Bill is doing his best to follow her logic. His wife reaches up and turns out the light again.

"It doesn't make you feel better?" ventures Bill. "It was supposed to."

❦

In the morning Bill gets up first, showers and kisses his sleeping wife on the cheek before heading off to work. His wife usually makes his lunch, but this morning he heads out the door empty-handed.

Being the first to arrive at the office, he sits at his desk for a while staring out the window in front of him. Without thinking about it, he scans the street, the curb and the embankment for cans before forcing his attention to his IN basket. Soon the others trickle in one by one. The receptionist walks in carrying the big bag of cans he left behind. Heading straight to his desk, she dangles the bag over his IN basket before letting it drop.

"So, do you want them or not?" the receptionist asks with her hands on her hips.

Bill doesn't want to talk about it right now.

"If you didn't want them, why did you come to my apartment in the first place?"

Bill just looks at her. He's trying to think of a way to make her shut up.

"He came over to my apartment last night," she tells the lady at the desk next to him. "He said he wanted my cans. They're in that bag. I give him all these cans when he comes over and he says, 'I got to go,' and leaves without taking them."

The lady is trying to take this in but is having difficulty. Bill is still considering his options.

"Doesn't that make you wonder why he came over in the first place?" the receptionist insinuates. "I mean, he is married, isn't he?"

Bill gets up and walks out the front door into the parking lot. It's cold and he doesn't have his coat, but it's better than in there. Finally he decides he should at least listen to what she's telling them. He walks back in and the receptionist is on the phone dealing with a customer. He goes to his desk and grabs the bag of cans before heading outside again. He finds the nearest dumpster and hurls them inside. I might as well throw my reputation in there also, Bill thinks.

When he returns to his desk, the receptionist is off the phone and the office is quiet. No one asks him to explain, but Bill can guess what they are thinking. The rest of the morning he keeps to himself, organizing his desk so at least something isn't a mess. Close to lunch time his wife calls, which is unusual.

"I thought I better remind you to be home on time tonight. We have dinner guests, remember?"

Bill knows. He's been dreading it. He is happy to hear from his wife, however. It's a good sign, he thinks. With his wife he doesn't say much; he lets her do the talking. He's not comfortable talking to her from his desk where everyone else can hear him.

"So, I spoke to your little receptionist friend," his wife continues. "We actually talked for about five minutes. She sounds pretty unhappy."

Bill can see the receptionist is looking at him.

"Yes," he says.

"She says you were a jerk to her this morning," his wife says, hoping he will fill in the rest.

"I have to buy my lunch," says Bill.

"Oh, you do? I guess so," his wife remembers. "I was going to get up and make it, but I was so tired."

"You needed your rest," Bill says.

"So, this receptionist," his wife starts again. "What's her name?"

"King Henry the Eighth," Bill says.

"What?" says his wife.

Bill doesn't say any more and there is an awkward silence. Finally his wife says, "Oh, can she hear you?"

"It's a home run, ladies and gentlemen!" Bill calls out in his best announcer voice.

"I'm sorry. I guess I'll do the talking. So you were a jerk to her," his wife says.

"I suppose so," says Bill.

"You did it for me?" his wife asks.

"It's what I do best," Bill says.

"I'm sorry about how I was last night. I do appreciate what you did," she says.

"So, tonight I get to look forward to an evening with dinner guests. What am I going to say?" asks Bill, suddenly feeling freer to talk. "I guess I might as well spill my guts about the cans."

"No," his wife recommends. "I wouldn't want it getting all over my work about you collecting cans. Would you do that for me?"

Bill looks over at the receptionist, at the lady next to him, out the window.

"Sure," he says. "Consider it done."

Jacqueline Windh

THE NIGHT THE FLOOR JUMPED

The window rattles. A train rumbles past, half-awakening me. For a moment I think I am back in my old apartment, above the railway tracks. But I live in this house in the forest now, no trains here. *Funny dream.* I curl deeper into my blankets to escape the sound.

But the rumble grows. The bookshelf makes a noise. My bookshelf! It vibrates, it clinks. Now I am abruptly awake, my body tense and humming like a guitar string. The bookshelf starts to slam against the wall above me, a crescendo of heavy beats. Suddenly everything on it cascades down upon me – my guidebooks, the two weighty volumes of the "concise" *Oxford*, the glazed clay rooster from Mexico. I try to sit upright as books spill off me.

This is it. This is it. Fear prickles the back of my neck. Knowing that I am supposed to "keep calm" only makes my heart pound faster. I glance around, but there are only moving shadows.

They warned us to keep shoes at the bedside. They said it could strike at any moment, that we are due.

Books pop up and down, their spines jabbing my ankles. I've been meaning to do that, keep my shoes at the bedside and a "grab'n'go" kit ready by the door. But my shoes are downstairs. I swing my feet to the floor.

I need to find my shoes. I can't run outside dressed only in this shirt; I need my robe.

But I cannot stand up. The room is swimming – I feel it rather than see it in the half-dark. The bed is starting to sway. I try to stand, but it jams my legs from behind and takes me out. The bookcase slams louder against the wall above me. *Forget the shoes, forget the robe, just get out.*

I slide across to Mark's side of the bed, slip to the floor and crawl on my knees through the hallway. The house is dancing me side to side, the floor jumping under me. I spread my arms wide in the corridor, but even so I am thrown against the wall. I keep crawling.

At the top of the stairwell, I turn to sit and brace myself, each arm pushed hard against the sidewalls. The force of the swaying takes me by surprise. I cannot get down the steps.

They warned us this could happen. In fact they said it *would* happen (some day), and that the shaking would be "severe." *The shaking.* I expected vibration, I envisioned wine glasses tinkling, perhaps even the odd window bursting and grazing me with shattered glass. Some cracks in the walls, a few trees down on the road.

But this is not shaking. This is the open sea. This is the worst ocean voyage imaginable. My home is a ship, tossed by seething waves of earth and stone. The beams are creaking. Dry dust cuts my nose and my throat. I feel sick. I need to escape this earth-storm, get down the stairs and out the door, out, far enough out. To where nothing can fall on me.

At the top of the stairwell, arms still braced against the swaying walls, I lower myself, *slow slow slow*, trying to create a third point of contact by planting my butt on the stairs. Fourteen stairs: I know this house. Just bump my way down fourteen stairs, then turn the corner to the door then out. That's all I have to do.

I've only made it to the third stair when the new noise starts. This is not the rumbling and rattling, or the groaning of the timbers; this is not the raging groundswell. This is more like the *crack* of an age-old cedar giant, the moment it tips and its trunk splits and it begins its slow fall through the forest. And suddenly I am coughing because there is more dust and things are falling on me and I can't move any more.

It is still. Dust is in my throat and I want to cough, but my side hurts if I breathe deeply. There are things on top of me. I don't hurt. Am I hurt? How long have I been like this?

It is dark, completely dark. It was night. I think it is still night. I think my eyes are open, but it is dark, so utterly dark.

I take a breath, a gentle breath. That doesn't hurt. Only if I cough. Why can't I move? If I was bleeding to death, would I feel it? Where are my hands?

I am lying on my back. Something hard jabs into my lower ribs. I try arching my body, squirming, but I am caught by a point of numbness somewhere around my left thigh, pinned like an insect in a specimen drawer. And what about my hands?

I clench the right. My fingernails cut into my palm. But I can't move the arm. It is splayed out beside me, held in place by something. But I can feel it. I clench the hand again, squeezing hard, then I try the left. It tingles, but it moves. This arm seems to be wedged under me, held there by my own body weight.

So now the legs. I can move the right one. There is room around it. I slide it side to side, then carve circles into empty space with my foot. I inhale, then return to the pinning point, where my left leg seems to end at the top of my thigh. I will the foot to move. But I can feel nothing. My ears start to pound and suddenly I am gasping for breath.

And now my stomach is convulsing and my side hurts again and I am gulping and wheezing. My leg, I want to know about my leg. Hot tears trace stinging tracks across my cheeks, and hang from my chin, tears that my pinned hands cannot wipe away.

My eyes are open now. Where there was black, there is now grey, a diffuse grey glow that filters through the wreckage of what was my house. Grey. Light. So it must be morning. Can I really have slept? I have to pee.

I wonder what Mark has heard. His plane would have landed in Houston hours before. With the time change, he would have been asleep, would have woken up to the news.

I try to see where I am, but it is hard to focus. Everything is too close, above and around me. Not much to see, as far as I can tell: A rough two-by-four, kinked and split where it landed upon another. Torn fragments of paint-flecked drywall, a reminder of what was. A twisted nail. A teaspoon.

Is he trying to get a flight back? Would he even come looking for me? I try not to remember how rigidly I stood as he kissed my cheek, his breath hot on my skin as he paused, waiting for me to speak or turn or relent, before he picked up his bag and walked away. How I watched, unmoving, as he reversed down the long gravel drive, pausing before the curve as he always does. How I closed the front door, its coolness on my forehead.

My bladder is full. I don't want to relieve myself like this, so I wait.

The grey light is growing stronger. Yes, it is morning. I cannot get a direct line of sight outside, not to the sky, nor to the cedar forest; but the abundance of light filtering through tells me that I am not buried deep. There is just enough on top of me to keep me from moving. If I can only get my arms free, perhaps I can push my way out.

But people will come for me. I need to hang on. This was a big one; it may be a day, perhaps two, before they get to me. I need to hang on, keep myself alive, till they come. They will come searching, soon. Surely. What must I do? What *can* I do?

I can move my hands. I clench the right and then the left. I can't feel the left hand anymore. It's only asleep, I tell myself. I squirm, I wiggle, I wedge myself upward to take the weight off that dead arm. Gradually, I am able to move it down, the back of my hand grating along the small of my back as I inch it down, all the while arching my body to relieve the weight, down and out and sideways. I ignore my swollen bladder, which aches each time I push upwards.

Finally, the arm is free. I try to clench my fist. I cannot see it or feel it, but it seems to move. I continue clenching and after a while the tingling starts, first the fingers and then moving up my arm, as the nerves crackle to life. The pain is exquisite.

I want to wipe my face, but there is not enough room to raise that free hand. My cheeks are tight where the tears dried. I squint, but that makes them prickle, threatening to make me sneeze. I cannot bear the thought of a sneeze right now; I am afraid its violence would kill me. I stop squinting, and think about the task of moving my left hand towards my face. But I save that for now, close my eyes to rest. There is time.

A rattling disturbs me. I awaken in terror; this time I cannot run. I wait for it to worsen, but it is gentle, a light shaking, like the spin cycle of that ancient washing machine Colette and I used to have. It is long over when I realize that I can release my breath and unflex my rigid limbs.

One of the drywall chips has fallen down, and rests at an angle on the board beside me, like a paint sample. I recognize it. *Forest fern*, the living room. Mark had wanted plain white; I was the one who wanted contrasts, who'd brought home colour wheels and curtain samples until he'd given in.

There seems to be more brightness to my left, so I twist my neck, angle my head. If I position it just so, I can catch a glimpse out with my left eye – a little tunnel through the debris aimed at the sky. It is all white, traversed occasionally by a darker grey band of cloud. I remain stretched to watch that bit of movement, even though it is awkward, even though my neck soon becomes sore and starts to burn. Eventually I spy a crow, a fleeting black speck against the white spot of sky.

The second aftershock is the strong one. It starts like last night, a sound that is at first without movement, like a distant approaching train. Then the vibration starts, and then the shaking. Something sharp pries into my back. I squeeze my eyes shut, hard, and hold my breath against the dust and wood-chips that rain down on me, and wait for it to stop. My left leg erupts in pain. *I can feel my leg.* I don't know whether that should bring joy or fear, so I simply revel in the sensation itself, the feeling of something, *anything*, sawing back and forth across my thigh.

The shaking stops. The sudden stillness unnerves me and I release my bladder. The stream of urine burns hot against the inside of my thighs. The smell is acrid and biting. I exhale, pushing the air out from the pit of my stomach, waiting for the stench to dissipate.

It's strange, I think, how much it sounds like a train. Last night, I thought it was a dream, that I was back in that old apartment with Colette. She still lives in that neighbourhood. The cities must have been hit, too. I wonder how she is, and I try to shut out the television images that come: apartment buildings collapsed, broken concrete, a dozen floors pancaked upon one another. Maybe that's why no one is searching here, yet.

The urine has dried on my leg, but its smell still hangs in the air, drifting up from the damp debris below. Now I am grateful that I am wearing only the night-shirt, no robe to hold the foulness against my skin. I stretch my neck to peek at my spot of sky, but it has disappeared, my little tunnel to daylight closed by this last shaking.

My eyes start to sting. How could this happen here? *Bodies pinned under the rubble.* Here, of all places! You'd expect this in Asia, in South America. But this is a first-world country for god's sake, how can this happen here? *A body pinned under the rubble.* That's me. For how long? I wonder. How long can people survive? How long will they keep searching?

My face crackles with dust, grit, dried tears. I return to the task of moving my left hand, so I can wipe my face.

The problem is that something is in the way. A board. I can flex my elbow, move my hand upward to a point, and then this thing is in the way. But it jiggles. I slide my hand up and down. Yes, it is a board, a two-by-four, I'd say. I can grip its splintery edge and jiggle it. Can I slide it? Yes, I can. I work on moving it end-on, down and away from me. Gentle jiggling, infinitesimal sliding. I am grateful that I have a task, something to work on. Something to occupy my time. And when my hand cramps, I am even more grateful that the task will be prolonged.

Jiggle and slide. Jiggle and slide. And when the hand cramps, take a break. Clench and unclench. Spread the fingers wide. Clench and unclench. Spread. Then take it from the top. Jiggle and slide.

Stop! I hear voices. Someone is out there. "Help," I call, "I'm here." But my voice is a mere croak, its reach deadened by the broken drywall and the rough boards. "I'm here, help me!" but I know they do not hear me and the sounds recede.

So I jiggle and slide, jiggle and slide.

The good news: I've managed to slide the board away. The bad news: it's started to rain. A drip falls on my face and trickles across my cheek. The good news: I can raise my left hand and wipe it away. Praise be for the small things.

I have never listened to a rain like this. My left ear is pressed hard against something that is cold and firm, and my right ear is open towards the sky. There are so many dimensions to the rain, to this rain, and I cannot believe that I have never been aware of them before: The distant hiss of all the rain, the thousands or perhaps millions of drops falling on the cedar fronds and on the lawn and on the driveway, an all-encompassing three-dimensional soundsphere that envelopes everything. But through that rises a two-dimensional rhythm, the patter on the remnants of my house above me, a gentle thrumming that speaks of a surface. And then, piercing through this is the pure singularity of a drip, a sharp *tunk tunk tunk* like a slow beat on a drum that creates the rivulet that trickles down the two-by-four above my face and lands on my cheek.

I brush it away.

A low rumbling sound pulses, growing, resonating in my chest, and I gasp as it thrusts me to wakefulness. Deep and rhythmic: it is a helicopter.

So someone is looking.

The light is dim and grey. It must be early morning. Dust sifts downward and I close my eyes. They are looking for us. The beating of the helicopter swells louder; it must be very low. A fleck of plaster lands on my cheek. There must be many of us.

What about Mark? Surely he is trying to get back here. I try to imagine what it is like out there, the airports, the roads. Maybe that's why no one has come for me. But surely Mark is coming.

Or maybe he is secretly relieved. I squeeze my eyes tight against the heat that flushes my cheeks and the throbbing in my forehead.

I think of the little girl at the next property over. They only moved in last month, she and her father. They had found the path through the trees that leads to our house. She was turning six, he'd said. He asked me to mind her this afternoon, he had an interview. Or that would have been yesterday, I suppose. Lisa. He asked me to mind Lisa for the afternoon. Are Lisa and her father waiting, like me, under the rubble?

The sound has faded, the helicopter has moved on. Rescuers, looking for signs of life? Or news crews here to broadcast images of this most recent disaster to the world? I wonder what they see.

My stomach hurts. My throat is dry, and my mouth. I close my mouth, breathe through my nose as I coax saliva to come, hoarding it, trying to build enough to swallow, to wet my sore throat.

The aftershocks don't scare me any more. I am even learning to categorize them. Most are very small, a few moments of vibration and then they fade. I do not have the same fear of them as before. Everything that can move or settle has already done so, so I squint my eyes tight against the dust that rains down on me and wait till they pass. There has only been one more strong one, and even that didn't frighten me until after, when I realized that this time I did not feel the pain in my leg at all. But even my leg, my leg, is a small price to pay, if only I get out of here.

The dull grey light seems to have brightened – or perhaps my eyes have simply adjusted to the dim light. I've been watching a beetle. I'm surprised by the intricate delicacy in its form. The legs are barely visible as it scuttles up and across the boards, but when it pauses with its antennae waving, I can see adornments on them: curves and spikes, with tiny upward curls at their ends instead of feet. The beetle paused once on a bright piece of drywall, and even in this dim diffuse light I could see hints of purple and green iridescence on its hard black shell. Its journey seems to be without purpose, up the piece of drywall along the edge of a board, then pausing as if thinking, changing its mind, then behind the board and out of sight. I look for it, and after a few minutes it reappears from under the same board, and scuttles up it and back, retracing the way from which it came.

The soft grey light *is* brightening. Perhaps it is afternoon. Or maybe the overcast is clearing. I survey my viewscape: The boards, the chips of painted drywall. It seems ridiculous now, the time spent choosing those colours. And the teaspoon, a fine sprinkling of white dust on it, like icing sugar, emphasizing the curled design on its handle. It's one of the few left from my childhood. My mother gave that old set, or what was left of it, to Colette and me when we started college. That spoon is as old as I am; I would have eaten from it when I was Lisa's age. I can see my little-girl hands curled around it, stirring my cereal and milk.

The beetle returns, running purposefully along the board, then down by my shoulder and out of sight. Suddenly it is on my face, those dry legs prickly on my cheek, my nose, my mouth. I jerk and spit; it crunches as I raise my free hand to swat it away. I catch my breath and watch for it, but it doesn't return.

I never thought that people who are pinned under rubble for days would actually sleep. I supposed I've never thought much about people pinned under rubble. I've seen them on the news from time to time as they are pulled out. But I've never thought about the days that preceded that moment of rescue. Now it is dark and I have awoken cold and wet and shivering; I can only conclude that I must have slept. Again.

So it's night once more. That means I have been trapped here for two days. It's a waiting game. I'm thirsty, and I realize that I've made one great mistake. All that work to be able to move my hand, so I could wipe away the water dripping on my cheek, falling just beside my lips. And now I am thirsty.

How long must people pinned under the rubble wait? I've heard the stories in the news many times: *Rescuers Continue Combing the Rubble for Survivors.* Then, after a couple of days, there are the miracle stories: the crying baby cradled in the arms of its dead mother dug up after three days unharmed; the octogenarian who survived for five. But after a week *Hopes are Growing Dim*, and soon the story shifts, to some other place, some other disaster. How many days?

Do I have any power in this?

They will come for me, I am sure they will. I must trust that they will. My job is only to stay alive, hang on and stay alive, be patient because surely I am not the only one. They have others to find. They'll get to me. Hang on.

Food, water, warmth. That's all I need, to hang on.

Food, I know, is all around me. The contents of my entire kitchen are now collapsed beside me. There are perhaps only a few feet of debris between me and a box of crackers or a tin of salmon. But it is all I can do to slide my left arm up or down. So I don't think of food.

Water, oh how I messed up! Flicking away that little dribble, rejecting that precious rain. Pray for rain, pray for more rain. I fight the tears, refusing to lose more water that way.

And warmth. I am cold and I am damp. I remember reading about a Buddhist monk who could control his body temperature at will. I didn't believe it. But now, I envision a fire burning deep in my belly, its incandescent heat growing in my core, radiating outward, and soon my beating heart is pulsing this warmth to my limbs, my fingers, even my toes and I am glowing, rapturous, buying time.

I lie here, watching, listening. After some time I am aware of an enveloping hiss, a sound that has started so imperceptibly that I am not sure if I am imagining it or not, until a trickle of water falls on my cheek. I tilt my head, grateful to feel the coolness in my mouth, grateful for the grittiness on my tongue and for the taste of plaster and sawdust.

The window shudders as the train passes on its nightly run. But this time, I awaken to silence. I blink, twice, if only to assure myself that my eyes are open.

The silence is immense, pounding. I try to remember the world I left, my world of – what, can it really be only two, no, three, days ago? That world that I could see and hear and feel and taste *oh to taste something, don't think, don't think*. My eyes are open wide, wider than they have ever been, my ears are pricked like a fox's, but there is simply nothing.

It is a gleaming sunny day. I know this because a needle of light stabs through my pile of rubble, and the incessant song of a wren pierces my solitude.

The irony strikes me, this carefree bird, no doubt perched on a bobbing hemlock frond and baring his innocent soul to the sun. I've tried not to think of what is going on in the greater world. What is the extent of the damage? The cities, the roads? How many others are trapped, besides me? Why have they not come for me? Perhaps there are no people left to rescue us. I've tried not to think.

And this little wren. Has he even noticed that things have changed? Or, on the scale of his world, his level of existence, is this merely a bit of landscaping? A few trees down but, really, still plenty of hemlock fronds to perch on, still plenty of bugs to eat.

I watch as the narrow sunbeam slides around. It starts at my left and makes its way in front of me, my small connection to the universe telling me that, yes, our planet is still spinning. And the wren is still singing when the beam makes its way to a piece of broken glass that glimmers for a moment, until the ray of light vanishes, its track intercepted by some larger piece of debris.

I need to keep my mind alert, aware. I wish for sleep, to pass the time. I think of things to think. I recite the passages of Shakespeare forced upon us in high school, whispering the parts I can remember and inventing the sections between.

A sound stops me: the clink of stones or metal. A soft shadow falls over my world. It is a dog, its breath rapid and loud as it thrusts its head into the rubble only a few feet from mine. The dog-smell in the warm dampness of its breath is stinky yet comforting. "Hey," I try to say, little more than a gasp. Its breath quickens and there is more clinking as it jabs its nose into the rubble, trying to reach me.

"Hey," I say again, and it pauses, letting out two soft, high-pitched cries. It can hear me.

"Dig." I urge it. "Come on, boy." It is silent, holding its breath, listening to me. I try to sound excited, enthusiastic. "Come on. Dig."

Then the panting resumes, and more clinking, and I hear it turn and trot away. I try to call it back, but my voice rises only barely above a whisper. I am left in silence once more. I want to believe that it is a rescue dog, that it's gone to tell them where I am. I so truly want to believe that.

I wait, and I listen. Normally, from my house, I can hear the traffic on the main road. But there is nothing.

My mother called me last week. Strange, like she'd known something was coming. I had been running out the door; I'd promised to call her back.

After some time, I smell a fire, the light scent of cedar smoke in the air. It is a comforting thought: probably people that I know, gathered together around it. The smoke lingers long in my nostrils, the scent itself indistinguishable from my memory of it.

I am tired of waiting. Where are they?

I want to turn over. My left shoulder aches and my arm has fallen asleep again. I want to be back in my bed, I want to feel the warmth of my flannel sheets. I want to be able to toss myself from one side to the other at will, to throw the blankets to the floor when I dream. It is too soon to die.

I wedge my arm back up, forward, move it up and down within its restricted range, until the pins and needles return and tell me yes, it's still there, it still works. I flex my other hand, my foot, checking in with each in turn.

If I could see Mark, if only for a moment. Just to tell him that it was me, it was never him.

I think I hear the call of an eagle in the distance. Another one answers, closer.

I wonder if the little girl hears them too. I cannot bear to think of her trapped like this. Little girls should not be caught under the rubble; they should be free to run around and play. I prefer to think of her with the others, around the fire.

The rain comes, soothing.

Another grey day. My wren returned, sang with the first light, but now he is gone. I think I can hear the wind, a rustle or a roar, but the water has stopped so it cannot be rain.

People are singing. I hear a chorus of voices rising, mingling with the whispering cedar fronds, the high notes losing themselves above the trees and the baritones rumbling the firmament below me.

Mark must have sent them. A parting gift.

I am tired of my view, so I close my eyes and listen to the music. Handel, I think, but I do not recognize the piece. Soon, night will come.

Then another voice comes in, dissonant and out of time. A man's voice. He is not even trying to sing! I was enjoying the music, this small pleasure (perhaps my last). Now I am angry. His voice continues, louder, now shouting, and I am outraged by his insolence, his selfishness, his disrespect. I want to yell to him *SHUT UP!* but my voice doesn't come, and my body can only vibrate with helpless rage.

Then my roof shifts and a trickle of grit falls on my cheek. The world turns searing white, and my eyes close tight from the stabbing pain as I feel the warmth of a human hand gripping mine.

Kris Bertin

TOM STONE
AND CO.

No job is harder than garbage.

Physically, I mean. There are plenty of jobs where you never lift a finger, though you may at any moment be subject to enormous pressures and stress. Bouncing, which I did for almost a decade, is that kind of job. Running a door, looking after a bar – you could go weeks without having to do anything more serious than carrying ice. Then, a moment of confrontation, where the wrong word, the wrong look might result in violence – or worse, disregard. A job like that is hard, and it's even harder if you treat physical confrontation as a last resort. Bars that don't want fights – that's the hardest. If you want to see a man under pressure, watch a bouncer talk a mean-looking guy out the door, watch him try to figure out the right combination of words that will dissolve the conflict into nothing. He'll be half-smiling, maybe pleasant, seemingly relaxed, but his pulse is picking up. Look at his neck. A vein, twitching. If they're good, they'll be rubbing their nose and pulling their ears, getting their hands up near their heads to catch a punch before it puts them out. They aren't scared, their bodies are just getting ready for something radically different from leaning against a wall and looking around. Hard work, but just for a moment, just until the guy's out the door.

But physically? As in your back and bones and hands and muscle? Garbage work is the hardest thing I've ever done. Sometimes it can take as long as 14 hours, like on holidays, when people's lives get swollen with stuff, when garbage bags have turkey corpses and wrapping paper and plastic blisters and what feels like whole human body parts in them.

I started the job because of my father-in-law. He drove a garbage truck for a private contractor, an old man who used to do it himself until he got too old and his knees stopped bending. Then Tom did it, taking in a sizeable chunk of the municipal contract, though the old man got the lion's share, driving and never getting out of the truck. The contract was grandfathered, Tom explained to me, so no corporate fucks could take it over and pay guys minimum wage for the hardest physical labor of their lives. The contract, which was for $110,000, would last until old man Sizemore retired or decided to renew it under a new guy. This is what my wife's father wanted, and what he eventually got when Sizemore didn't show up one day (because he was dead).

Of course, he died without working anything out with city council, but they came to Tom with a job offer anyway. The wrinkled old veterans and retired schoolteachers who made up the council had a serious hate-on for corporate fucks too, and told GARBCO and Vigilant Cleanup to stay the hell out of their municipality. Tom Stone was on the job.

I'd helped him with the job before, like any son-in-law would, working as hard as I could possibly go, not complaining, not slowing down for anything. And when I finished, he'd give me a wad of cash which I would refuse – then he'd insist and I'd refuse again – back and forth until I'd accept or he'd smuggle it home in my wife's purse. Then I'd go back to my job, bouncing, and I'd thank Christ I wasn't doing garbage full-time. My back so stiff and sore that it felt like something was broken back there.

Then, one morning, Tom called me. Offered me a job. Three days of work a week for 5 grand. Said he wanted to offer it to me before he got some punk he didn't even know to do it.

I asked for time to think about it and he said he wanted my answer in two days. When I hung up, I knew I was going to take the job. It was too much money for too little work – I couldn't pass it up. Even still, I could feel it, feel all the aches and pains that were coming. I could almost see them, waiting to fill my body, waiting for me outside my window like cartoon ghosts.

Kelly didn't know if it was a good idea, but she said that she'd be happy to see me helping her father. Thing was, Kelly wasn't going to leave her job and move back to her home town, so I suggested that maybe I could drive there and do it, since it's only two hours away. What I didn't say was that it would be nice to get away from each other for a few days each week, but I knew she was thinking it too. Bouncing kept me at home the exact same hours as her, though I'd slip out in a coat marked SECURITY just as she was drifting off to sleep. She worked at a private school from 8 a.m. until noon, which was the exact time I would wake up with a hard-on, get mad that she's not home yet, and roll back over. For some couples, it's money or family or neighbours or some other thing that made them fight. For us, it was sex. The sex I wanted that I wasn't getting, and the sex I was dishing out that she didn't need.

And honestly, the job made it work. My little trips three days a week made it so I was exhausted by the time I got back, and the day before, I left so early that I had to be in bed before she even finished reading her paperbacks. Magically, we were on her once-or-twice-a-week-is-more-than-enough schedule, and I was more or less satisfied. Your body changes, of course, and can adjust itself to almost anything. My balls went from squirrely little maniacs to big, lazy guys, asleep on my thigh. I'd feel a dull throb every now and then, but it had to contend with a roaring, groaning throb in my lower back, and my back would always win.

And it wasn't like I was having fun while I was away. Tuesday-Wednesday-Thursday I was sleeping in the double bed that my wife had slept in as a girl, the room kept exactly the same as it was back in the 80s. Try masturbating with a wall of stuffed animals in front of you, in a lacy bed with your mother and father-in-laws snoring just feet away in the other room. Maybe some people could. I did it only four times – and I remember each of them distinctly. Each time I promised myself it was the last time until I finally agreed with myself and stopped midway through, stopped for good.

Every now and then it would occur to me that I was a grown man with a wife who I was supposed to be starting a family with, spending more waking hours with her father than with her. But these thoughts had trouble sticking because in truth, I was happy. Tom and I got along better than I did with my real father, and we were similar enough men that we could spend hours together in the enclosed space of the truck and still get along. We were similar enough that you could proba-bly make some kind of Freudian claim about girls mar-rying their fathers if you wanted to, but you wouldn't be exactly right. Maybe I was the kind of man Kelly *thought* she wanted, but three years into our marriage, and I could tell she wasn't so sure anymore. Something about my unfulfilled promises about college, about my shitty jobs, and (like I said) our out-of-sync sex drives. And maybe something big and nameless about ambition and success and status. One time, when we fought about it, she said I could've been anything.

An other time, she said *men are animals.* After a minute she said she didn't mean me.

When I was home, I took walks and smoked cigarettes when Kelly wasn't around and chewed gum when she was, and more than once she came home to find me in bed, face-down and drunk. I lifted weights I didn't need to be lifting, and took to hanging out at my old bar – not bouncing, but sitting on a barstool through the day-shift and talking to the bartenders, waiting for some action to come my way, though it never did.

And other times I would have a surge of emotion or love for my wife and I'd end up trying to cook some big, complicated thing for dinner to surprise her with, though only once did it turn into sex. And even then I had to do so much and it took so much effort and planning that it almost wasn't worth it. Then I started doing it so much she figured out what I wanted when I made a nice meal, and that pretty much ended it. After that my eggplant parmesan with asparagus or grilled portobello (with gnocchi and roasted red peppers) would get dumped into a casserole and left on the counter, even if she watched me prepare the whole thing. Then I'd go do something stupid instead of talking to her, like trying to chop down a tree on our lawn or bench 250 pounds (by myself).

The first few months I was slinging trash I called her every night I spent away. Then, when I realized I always called *her*, I stopped to see what would happen, and she never made an effort. It became like I was married Friday through Monday, and the rest of the time I was a big teenage boy apprenticed to a master garbage-man, sleeping in his daughter's pink room. Sometimes, when he would mention her, I would imagine that she was promised to me, but we hadn't officially started our marriage yet. That would come later, when I was a journeyman garbage guy and I would be given my own garbage barony to run.

∞

The job was changing my body fast. My biceps shrunk and my forearms grew. My back too. My back was the big one, totally overdeveloped from throwing the garbage bags overhand into the truck. We didn't have one of those big crushers and a handy pole to hang off the back with – we had a modified cube truck with multiple gates across the back; a real do-it-yourself job left over from Old Man Sizemore. A small-town rig. Tom always talked about getting a real truck, but it was one of those things that just never materialized. This was either because we couldn't afford it, or because Tom appreciated the challenge that the inefficient system presented to us.

As the trash piled up in the back, you'd shut the first gate to keep it in, then the gate on top of that, then the third one. And by then you were throwing a bag that might weigh up to 15 pounds, throwing it overhand, trying to get it to follow the perfect arc and go *swish* into the back, some 12 feet up. Tom Stone was 60, but he could do it better than me, could always get it on the first try. And a bag of trash and diapers and wood stove ash never burst open on his head, ever. That sort of thing could only happen to me, and it didn't matter that I was younger and stronger and outweighed Tom by 65 pounds. Then again, Tom had none of my flattening skills, and if he was the one to climb up into the back to squash everything down, he could stomp with all his might but it would never give more than a couple inches.

And that was the job. Drive, stop. Get out, get trash. Throw it – stomp it down if you really have to. Again and again and again until it's over. Of course, when someone really dropped the ball garbage-wise, Tom Stone would go and knock at their door, whatever time it was. That was part of the job too. Or at least what Tom thought was part of the job. He'd always tell me to wait in the truck, so I'd never get to hear what he'd say. I'd see him point a lot. At himself, the truck, at the mangled TV, or the queen-sized box spring they were trying to pass off as haulable trash.

I always wanted to do that part of the job with him, because it was something I knew I was good at, but he said it was more important that one of us stayed behind. Who knows what the hell these people are capable of, he'd say. And he was right, I think. Some parts of the run, the really broken-down parts, could give you that feeling, the one where you know you've entered into something you want no part of. A lady with a baby that's screaming *too* hard, or an old man living with a young boy that Tom says isn't his grandson. It's not that country people are more fucked up than anyone else; it's just easier to see the really damaged people when they're on a big tract of land with lots of windows instead of a high-rise apartment with locks and curtains and no yard to speak of.

The most screwed up were the Cliftons. One of those huge families on a piece of land that had been in the family for generations. People who had a farm but did no farming. They always had too much trash for us to take, sometimes as much as twenty bags, but we never said anything about it. There was just too much wrong with the place – trash everywhere, all around their run-down bungalow and in the grass and trees and hanging from the scrubby bushes peppered across the place. There were broken beer bottles and dogshit and blown-out tires. You got the idea that it would be easier to just take the extra load and move on.

It was always bad there, but the worst – the very worst we saw – was on a Tuesday morning, at maybe seven o'clock. It was strange to see anybody awake on that leg of our run, but there they were – 12 of them – great big people in lawn chairs and kitchen chairs, sitting around a burnt out fire-pit. It was a party that hadn't ended, and they were still going, drinking and smoking cigarettes and dope even as the sun came up and their kids needed to get to school.

They were far enough away from us that we didn't have to talk to them, but they waved and shouted for us to come over. Tom shot me a look and we acted like we didn't hear, gathered up their cans in silence. He'd always say it wasn't worth it to talk to them, and when I saw them that day, I could see what he was getting at. Even though the garbage run was in a different county than the one we lived in, we'd still heard of the Cliftons, still knew what people said about them. It was your standard fare – diddling kids, smacking women around, getting arrested all the time for all kinds of stuff. It didn't matter if they used grocery bags instead of the real trash bags, it didn't matter how much they dumped on us. They were the kind of people you didn't even want to *see*, let alone talk to.

That day, we thought we were getting off scot-free when one of them – a fat teenage girl in a nightie – ran for the tree line, holding her crotch and mouth at the same time while the family laughed and laughed. Tom turned away for the driver's side, but I saw her crouch down and lift her skirt in front of everyone, and at the exact same time, fire a jet of green vomit out her mouth like a laser beam. And everyone laughed even harder. Tom and I drove away after that.

These fucking people, Tom said.

I remember as we went to the next lot that he had a look on his face that wasn't exactly anger or sadness or even concern, but he kept shaking his head and saying *fuck*. At the time, I guessed it was about the kids, because they had a ton of them, and because I knew he'd grown up in the same kind of situation. I realize now that he was probably just trying to look at them and decide how many degrees of *fucked-up* there were between him and them.

∞

I could feel it coming between them and us. Could feel something there that we would get drawn into just by being near it – just by *driving past*. If I hadn't worked on the door, I wouldn't know what it was. If I was another person, it would've just been a feeling of un-easiness and nothing more. But it had been my job to look at people and know who we were on a collision course with, my job to watch. To be ready for this kind of stuff.

At the bar, they were usually the people on their way to being regulars, trying their hardest to be liked and make friends with the staff. You could always see the ways things would go wrong coming right at you and there was usually nothing you could do about it. Nothing until that moment happened where they pushed it too far and said or did whatever it was that made it so I had to step in or get waved over or whatever. Sometimes they knew it was coming too, but most of the time they couldn't know the most basic truth: that no matter how much they talked to me or clapped me on the back and called me "pal" – we weren't friends. Then I'd say or do whatever I'd have to, and there'd be a moment where they decide what kind of man they were, how far they would want to take it. This is the moment where most people get adrenaline dumped into their bloodstream and they get crazy. If you were on the door, this was the moment you were waiting for. It was the moment you got paid for, the whole reason you're there. It was the moment that erased all the other stuff like waiting around and checking IDs and helping old ladies down the stairs. It took root in your brain and became the one thing you remember about that night months later.

Some people would swear revenge for being thrown on the street, for having the inseam of their jacket ruined, for suffering the insult of being told never to come back. Only once did anything ever come of it

– from a guy named Cal that I had kicked out years ago.

Kelly and I had driven out to the beach – to the Atlantic – and we were trying to find a place to lay down our blanket. He wasn't looking for us, obviously – there was no way he could've known we were planning to come there. It was just the hottest day of the year and half the city was there, including him and his lowlife friends, smoking and drinking on the far side of the beach in all the scrubby grass.

I didn't see him, but I got that feeling, that bad-dream, something-is-behind-you feeling when he threw the first beer bottle. It sailed past Kelly's head, sprayed us both with beer, then landed in the sand with a thunk and hissed itself empty. I put on my shoes, even before turning around. Later, Kelly would say that this was the scariest part to her – that I knew what I was going to do to him immediately. That I knew I needed shoes for it. And most of all, she said, was that I did it automatically, like it was something I couldn't control.

When I turned around and stood up, he was maybe 20 feet away from us and grinning, his swollen belly hanging over his shorts, rising and falling while he decided what his next move was. He had another beer in the other hand, unopened, and I remember that it was like he couldn't decide whether to drink it or hand it to me, or try to throw that one too. The last thing he said was *Remember me, asshole?*

I didn't say anything to him. I just went forward while Kelly started to scream my name and everyone started to watch.

∞

It's a bad day. Tom and I are both extra sore because yesterday was a particularly huge haul. To cope, we'd gone drinking. Some guys had tried to start shit with Tom and he'd gotten so pissed he took me to a different bar and we got even drunker. I had no problem stepping up to a bunch of fat 50-somethings, but Tom wouldn't let me. I didn't know what they said to him, and I got the sense Tom didn't want me to ask. I really wanted to though – the way they'd been looking at us was like they thought we were a pair of child molesters. Then the next bar was closing and we had to get up pretty much as soon as we'd gone to bed and now it was too cold and too sunny and our backs are pounding as hard as our heads.

It's the day we have to talk to Cliftons. We pull up to a swing set with cracking blue paint, enormous with thick metal poles – the kind you'd find at a school – and still assembled. The thing has each one of its legs in a trash-can, which are filled with garbage, too. It looks like it would've take a lot of work and planning to even get the swing to the end of their driveway, let alone into the cans. It's all half in the snowbank, towering over us, its chains clinking like wind chimes.

This is too big, Tom says.

Stay here, I tell him.

No, he says. I'll talk to them.

But he doesn't move. He puts his hands on his hips and takes a deep breath instead.

Stay here, I tell him again, and this time he doesn't disagree.

Then I'm marching up the driveway in my dark-green jumpsuit, trash blowing around like tumble-weeds, and even though it's completely different from working the door, I feel like I know exactly how this will turn out because I've done this a 100 times. I can even feel that same old feeling of knowing that I'm going to be doing something that needs to be done, a thing that no one, including me, wants to do.

I hear Tom call after me that he's going to stay in the truck, and I just wave my hand without turning around. I'm up and onto their porch. It's a mess of trash and snow and ice and bloated old couches, two busted fridges, and a giant set of aluminum blinds that are twisted and wrapped around everything. Somewhere, a dog starts barking.

The oldest Clifton, Tobias, introduces himself and invites me in but I don't go in. Instead we stand on either side of the doorway with the cold air blowing into his house and the bad smell blowing out. He's old and smoking and looks like he could be dying on his feet. His face looks like a solid thing, like when all the moisture leaves a mud puddle and it becomes that hard stuff with those deep criss-crossed trenches.

He tells me that the swing set was put out last night by the boys, and that he told them I wouldn't take it. Says it so as to sound like he's on my side. Then he asks me where Tom is, like they know each other.

We can take five bags of trash, I tell him. A household this big, I can do a bit more, but that's it.

Yeah?

I point to the truck.

It's a small truck. Five bags. I can't take your swing set.

Leave it there then. Teach the boys a lesson, he says, then gives me a smile I don't like.

I will, I say. But I can't take your trash today.

The old man looks at me, and there's no sound but the wind for a little while. No smell, except for him. Then that dog starts to bark again.

You got to take the trash, he says. You *got* to. We got 14 fuckin people here. You're just mad about the swing.

Are *you* gonna go wrestle that thing out of your cans?

It's the law, he says, and I can see something building up in his head, in his eyes.

I can't take the swing, *or* your trash. Do you understand?

This isn't right, he says. You people just think you can do anything.

There's another long moment of him looking at me. Me, looking away and at their lawn. A hole, half-dug, the pile of earth beside it frozen solid. A half a motorcycle in the hole. That same old feeling of weighing things comes on and I give him one more glance before I decide this isn't worth it.

When I leave and head up the road, I swear I hear him call me something. It's *cocksucker* but it's just the faintest, weakest *cocksucker* I've ever heard and it gets caught in the wind and blown up and away.

I stop walking when I hear it, and before I turn around, I hear the door shut.

∞

At the beach, Cal didn't end up throwing the second beer.

He ended up running away with it in his hand, like he forgot it was there. When I got him, he was near those rocks wrapped in chain link that divide road and beach, and he was trying to find the fastest way up in his bare feet. When I threw him down, he managed to hang onto the bottle, and it didn't even bust. It busted when I stomped on it, and only then did he realize what he'd done. He was trying to think of something to say, like *stop* or *call the cops* when I wrenched his arm up behind his back. Then I stomped on that, too. Then he couldn't say anything, or at least nothing I could understand.

It seemed so clear that this would be the result of his actions. It seemed so simple and pure and basic and I didn't understand why he would do it. Why he couldn't understand what outcome would pour out of that moment when he cocked his arm and threw a bottle at my wife. I had liked the idea of leaving without saying anything, but I couldn't.

What did you think would happen here?

He didn't have any answers for me – he just rolled around and sobbed and moaned – so I just left him there.

I think about it a lot. About him and me. There were other bad ones, bad showdowns and standoffs, and he wasn't even the worst one. But somehow my mind would always end up back there, the both of us in shorts, me standing over him with my boots. The in-and-out of the water and the wind. Him and me.

Kelly and I do one of those things people do when they try to pretend everything's okay. When you're trying to fix things without wanting to admit anything's broken. It's maybe a year into my garbage career and we haven't spent very much of my salary, so there's talk of a trip. She tells me she thinks it would maybe be good for us to *get to know each other again*.

It sounds like one of those meaningless new-age things when it comes out of her mouth, but as it bounces around in my head it takes on new meaning. The memories of getting together, of falling in love are getting dull and weird. A few times I would even remember them wrong, remember whole events and conversations that never happened, and there is even one moment, just a few seconds long, where I remember my marriage proposal wrong. I remember it taking place in her dumb little bedroom, the one I sleep in three times a week instead of the cheap hotel room I did it in, the one we promised to visit every anniversary. It's even getting easier to remember nights on the door, nights as a single man surrounded by women, all of them too drunk, all of them trying too hard to catch my eye. Getting easier to remember the bar without her in it, even though she was the whole reason I'd stayed at the job in the first place.

It's scary because it felt like a whole part of my life was something that happened to me, instead of something I took part in. I would go back and forth between thinking that I really didn't know her anymore, and that I *never* knew her. Some days I would re-dedicate myself to our marriage, and others I would think, but never say: it's over. These thoughts come to me, both in our bed and hers, both as I lay next to her and lay alone, staring at a stuffed California Raisin clutching a plastic saxophone.

When *our trip* comes up again, I tell Kelly I can't really take time off, so she goes above my head, talks to her father directly. He brings it up the following week, when we're at the dump, tipping the truck's hydraulics into the sorting centre, with that awful safety beeper going off and on.

It's no big deal for me, Tom says, sucking on a cigarette. For the two weeks you're in France, I'll get one of
Kelly's cousins to fill in.

France, I say.

Paris, he says.

It's both the first I've heard about Paris, and the first
time I ever disagreed with Tom. It's just that there's no
way I can tell him I don't want to go. Right then and
there he calls up his little nephew on his cellphone, starts
making plans.

And so we do all the things you're supposed to do in
Paris. Walk along the Seine, scope out the Louvre and
the Bastille and the Eiffel Tower. Do everything but
fuck, of course. Despite the fact that people are making
out in the street, trying to act out their Hollywood fan-
tasies about Paris, her and I walk hand-in-hand, and
sleep in a spooning position with me on the inside so I
don't get hard in the night and start bucking my hips
against her ass.

Drunk on wine and cheap French beer under the
Arc de Triomphe, I put my hands up her dress and she
asks why sex is all I care about. The best answer I can
give her is *I care about you*, and while it's mostly true, it's
only one part of a whole bunch of moving pieces and
feelings.

Still, it works, and back at the hotel, we fuck like we
did when she was a waitress saving up her tips for school
and I was the bouncer staying late just to hit on her. We

roll around and hold each other's faces and say I love you more than usual. But the next day, the next week, it's like it never happened. She doesn't touch me again until our final night, and even then, we don't do anything interesting, nothing particularly Parisian – and it's over in the usual half-hour.

I want to tell her that when she went to see the Catacombs and I stayed behind, I wasn't feeling sick. I stayed behind to jerk off to bad French porn on the television, to empty myself of all the anger and cruel words I might say to her. I want to tell her, as she's drifting off to sleep, that it didn't work, that it just made everything so much worse.

Later, when she shows pictures of the piles of skulls and femurs to the neighbours and her friends, she mentions how scared I was in those tunnels. She even says I was shaking. I realize that maybe this is what marriage is about: believing whatever you want to believe about a person – making up your own happy stories and laying them over top of whatever ugly or ordinary thing actually took place.

∞

There's a phone call we get that makes it so we have to board our transatlantic flight days early. It's about Tom.

As Kelly lays her head on my shoulder to try and get some sleep and I watch stacks of clouds come up and around our plane, Tom Stone is sitting with his wife in the ER, having his EKG results read.

While I'm reading the same single laminated sheet about in-flight safety and emergency landings over and over again, Tom is in a gown, waiting to hear about the contents of his blood.

When I'm getting a stupid, uncontrollable hard-on both because of Kelly's head in my lap, and the 20-something without a bra in the seat ahead of us, Tom is having the first CT scan of the day, his blood filled with green radioactive dye.

The phone call was about how Tom had collapsed, face down in a snowbank on the last leg of the garbage run. About how Kelly's little cousin Eddie freaked out and ran a half-mile to the next house for help, despite having access to the garbage truck, his cell phone, and Tom's. Later, when I take over the garbage run, cousin Eddie tells me that when he turned Tom over, his eyes were blank and staring up at the sky like his soul had left his body.

Like a fucking dead guy in a movie, Eddie says, fiddling with his phone in the passenger seat. Scared the shit right outta me.

The phone call we received was about how Tom and Judy needed us back ASAP, because no one knows what's wrong and there was no way to tell if it was going to turn out to be nothing or something *bad*.

I think, if we wouldn't have gotten that call, things could have been different. I would have my mind made up about leaving her. Kelly wouldn't be clutching me the whole time, and I wouldn't be worried, feeling the invisible stuff that connects me and someone who should be a stranger, someone who is as much a part of me as a blood relative. Instead I'm wrapped up in some sense of belonging and urgency and when I look at my wife all of my escape plans and big ideas fly out of me, out of the plane and into the Atlantic like lost luggage.

∞

The first week Tom is in the hospital, I take over the run. The whole system is fucked though, because now Kelly is down, and the two of us have her parent's bed instead of the little pink one. Now my job is to console her, try to get her to stop crying and convince her everything is going to be okay, if only so I can actually fall asleep before the sun is stinging my eyes open. Now, my time is divided between the hospital, the run, and holding Kelly's terrified body.

Tom tells me they have no idea what's wrong with him. None. And they can't figure it out.

Stress, Tom says. It's fucking stress is what they're saying.

Tom, I ask him, what do you have to be stressed out about?

He doesn't say anything and neither does Kelly and for a minute I think I'm just being an asshole just by the way they're looking at each other. Then Kelly takes me in her arms and begins to cry again, while Tom's head turns stiffly and looks out the window by his hospital bed.

Mornings are hell, and I have to drive, because Kelly's cousin Eddie is usually so burnt-out he can't even stay on the road, much less stop at the right point to line up the truck with the trash. Without Tom, almost anything that made me like the job is gone, and I have to do my work, plus Tom's. Between every stop, it's Tom I think about, along with phrases like *incurable illness* and *a death in the family.*

As we make our way to the very first house to start the run, Eddie likes to read fucked-up headlines to me. He gets them on his cell phone, so they're just little blurbs without much detail – the gist and that's it – and he reads them like they're big, unbelievable secrets, even though there are literally hundreds of these things.

MAN DIES OF INTERNAL BLEEDING
FROM SEX WITH HORSE

STUDENT KILLS TEACHER WITH PROJECTILE-
WEAPON CONSTRUCTED IN CLASSROOM

THIEF (26) STEALS AND SWALLOWS A DOZEN
DIAMOND RINGS IN DEPARTMENT STORE

I wanted to take the diamonds, Eddie says in a funny voice, *but I also just wanted to see if I could swallow that many.*

Then he looks over at me like I'm supposed to be impressed.

He reads them to me with such consistency it ends up feeling like morning announcements at school, so I just drive and smoke and try to imagine that I'm learning important information. Eddie would interject between sips of Red Bull, usually to add useful tidbits like *that's nuts*, or *Christ*, or most often, *People are fucked.* This, I decided, was the driving force behind all the headlines. It was something big, the kind of question you ask yourself your whole life, something between *what's wrong with people*, and *why do we do any of the things we do?* I take the headlines as a friendly reminder that things are never going to be as good as we want them to be. That the best you can hope for are the long valleys of peace between moments where someone takes off all their clothes at the library and starts knocking over bookcases.

One morning I ask him if he can get the real news so him and I can actually know what's going on. He surprises me by saying *man, nobody knows what's* really *going on.*

When him and I first see the Clifton farm, the swing set's still there, along with those old couches from my visit to the porch. trash bags piled around it, maybe 20 or 30 – last week's and this week's – and a few of them are blown open, or maybe torn open by animals. As we pull up, we see two men standing out there, smoking cigarettes in winter jackets while paper and wrappers and plastic bags flutter around them. A black dog sitting next to one of them. A big dog, bloated and all head, just like them.

There's a moment where I nearly stop. A moment where I nearly get out and give them what they want, but it's too early, I'm too tired, and I have too much work to get done. One of them is holding something. Maybe a stick, or a pipe. I know exactly how I'd take it from him, and what would happen once I did.

Eddie's just out of high school and still lives with his parents. When I ask him what he's thinking about doing with himself, he talks about becoming a policeman and his voice gets stiff and strong. I can maybe see the kind of man he'd have to become in order to make that happen, but when we see the Clifton boys waiting for us that day, his voice is quiet, soft. He asks *what was that*, like he'd seen something he couldn't even understand.

It's the first time we ignore them, roll right past their driveway and onto the next house.

Then one day, Tobias waits for me, alone, at the end of the drive, next to the huge pile of trash.

I stop and roll down the window. We don't say much. It's gone too far now. Now, I'm saying that I'm not collecting trash because I was threatened, and he's saying I was threatened because we weren't collecting trash.

You'd better smarten up, he tells me. You're in for it.

I tell him I'll see what I can do about it.

Your brain's just as scrambled as his, he says.

Who? I ask.

That fucking *animal* Tom Stone, he spits.

I don't get him to elaborate. After that, we don't take trash from the Clifton house anymore. We drive right by them every week, and that's it. A few times, the guys are out there, and one time they even throw something at us – a bottle – and it smashes on the road behind us. Their trash pile gets bigger and bigger until it splits in two, divides and multiplies over the weeks like something under a microscope.

∞

We lose the contract before Tom's even out of the hospital.

It's my fault, and everyone knows it, though no one says anything. Eddie and I both have to have surgery for the same thing in different places – to have tendons reattached in our hands and wrists. His is worse than mine, but my surgery is more invasive, the doctor says. Still, it's Eddie that got the most stitches, Eddie who had to get fingers sewn back on. I don't think of it as being my fault at first, but little by little I can see it across Kelly's face, and even Eddie's, though he swears he doesn't regret it. Says it was worth it. Only Tom calls me a hero, and thanks me for protecting Eddie. Tells me every time he shuffles from his hospital room to mine. He seems totally unaware that I've drastically altered our lives.

You're obsessed with these people, Kelly had said to me before it happened, in the weeks leading up to it when I was really worked up about the whole situation.

I didn't bother arguing because there wasn't any sense in it. She didn't believe me that anyone had been calling and hanging up on us, or that it was the Cliftons, or that the same thing had been happening to Tom for a while. She didn't believe that they'd actually tried to start something with us, or that I had to do something about it, but then she never did think that about anything.

Afterwards, I see the events like a grocery list, one thing on top of the other, one thing pushing into the next, each of them absolutely unavoidable. It all had to happen, because it did, another automatic situation:

Us.

Driveway.

Kids.

Dog.

Eddie's hand.

My hand.

Truck.

Hospital.

We're there on our day off – Eddie and me – after one last driveway encounter. City council said we *had* to take their garbage. Now, it was a health hazard, and so we went there at the end of our run. Tobias had compromised, and the swing set was disassembled, even though the poles and joints were still too heavy, too big for us to take. There was enough trash to fill the entire truck, and we already had the first gate shut when the whole family came out. The sons and their wives or sisters or whatever the fuck they were, and Tobias, of course.

This time, he says we can't take it. He says he didn't want us to anymore.

Are you serious? I ask him.

You faggots hit the road before we call the fucking cops, he said. You two *get*.

It was pretty smart, actually. He'd talked to the city and they'd agreed to have us take it. Now, if we didn't do it, the family could say we just didn't come, and that would be it for us. Our solution was the come early, at quarter to four in the morning. Load it all up before they even knew it. We were there to do our job, to fig-ure out a way to end this thing, but I'll admit we were also there to fight. I was ready to take on the big one and his brother, was thinking about how I'd do it. But running an idea through your head as many times as it'll go doesn't mean it will happen. It doesn't mean anything.

Are you ready? I ask Eddie. He puts on his policeman voice and says *hell yeah*.

When we get to the driveway, it isn't very long before the door opens and that black dog shoots out. The door closes after that, and no more people come out. It's too fast, and at first I don't even know what I'm looking at. Just a black thing, low to the ground, coming at us, like a tiny storm cloud.

It's over in maybe three minutes, but it feels longer. It feels like it takes forever to get to the moment where there's no new pain, no movement or those deafening sounds, all piled on top of each other. Then it's me and Eddie and the dog. Then it's just red snow and what's wrong with us now. Rows of bite marks up my entire arm, but Eddie's got the worst of it. His hand doesn't look like a body part. It looks like a lasagna that fell on the ground. He's laughing instead of crying or screaming, like maybe he can see some humor in this that I can't.

I lie down for a while after that, next to Eddie and the dog and the three of us make up one whole, one single thing. Slowly I notice more parts – little figures filling the windows of the house. Children watching us. It's when I finally get up that I realize there aren't any trucks or cars here. They're here by themselves. That's when I realize it. The kids opened the door.

There's no way to know if it was their idea or if they were told to do it, but I could see how it would happen. Them, watching us pull up, talking amongst themselves. Taking the dog by the collar, or maybe it follows them down the stairs, through that house with all of its smells. Creeping up to the door in sock feet. Opening the door in one go so that it's over and done with. I wondered if it was the youngest or oldest that would do it, or if it didn't matter who did it. I can see them lining up in the windows, their heads poking up over the sill in the cold room of the porch like 10 little Indians.

The dog gets Eddie, then I get the dog, then the dog gets me. I kill it. I do it by pushing my hand all the way down its throat while it bites me all the way up my arm, tears me right open.

When we leave the farm, I take the dog's body with me. Eddie asks me why, holding his hand up in front of him like a dead fish, the finger missing from it in his other hand, and I tell him I don't know, it's just what happened.

∞

When I get fired, the question I'm asked is *what were you doing there?* That's the big one, though they of course say they have to bring up the fact that Tom's one of those guys with two families – a regular one and a secret one. When I hear it, I immediately know which less-than-reputable group of people would have brought these facts to the council's attention. I get the idea that the Cliftons might have made up a lie about us that was actually true about *their* family. It's not the whole city council that meets with me, just the indignant, moral-high-ground ones most offended by the city's employment of Tom Stone and Co.

Eddie's with me, the both of us with bandages and braces and wraps, and I immediately regret having him meet me here. He's wearing a big hoodie with a bunch of shiny metallic shit on it and a big hat with a straight bill. I tell them that it's nothing but a bunch of unsubstantiated bullshit and that they can't fire us for rumors, but Eddie's long, bare neck and bloodshot eyes destroy my words as they hit the air. He smells like weed and vomit and it looks like he's been self-medicating on top of the codeine they prescribed for us.

The fact is, one of the councilor says, you aren't on the books. Not officially. You're floating right now until we fully renegotiate. All of this was done informally.

Are you seriously going to believe this stuff? I ask them. These are serious allegations. Crazy allegations.

I don't care about that stuff, one of them says. She doesn't look as mad as the other ones. She looks like a televangelist in her red pantsuit. I just want to know why you were *there* at four in the morning.

I already explained that, I say, then elbow Eddie, but he's too hung-over to back me up.

There was no reason for you to be there. If they wouldn't let you take it, you should've called us.

Then one of the real fire-and-brimstone guys gets in my face and starts saying stuff about how we're a disgrace and an embarrassment, and I just look at him. He stares at me with righteous fury like he's looking into the eye of Satan and I think about how this was probably an important moment for these people. To them, it's a big part of *their* story, the moment where they ousted the crazy garbage guys for the good of the city.

Every word that comes out of their mouth throbs in my head and lower back. There's no getting around it. We're fired. Tom's fired. They don't want any of us.

I take Eddie and leave and all three of them stand so they can watch us leave. There's a feeling of vertigo, like my inner-ear is gone screwy when I get to the front doors and I can still feel their gaze on me. When I hear one of them say *these people*.

When I tell Tom, he's so mad and sick and frustrated, he just begins to cry. It's almost an unbearable thing to watch, and I try not to look at him when he breaks down and begins to shake. It's all over in a matter of moments though, and he's clearing his throat after that, saying *sorry, sorry*.

It's after the meeting that I realize I have a dead dog in my car. The only place I can think to put it is at the

Clifton's, but I know I can't go back there. I realize that there is no reasonable place to put a dead dog, so it goes in a large dumpster behind city hall.

∞

Cal had been kicked out of Ron's a few times, but the one that got him thrown out for good – the one that led to the thing on the beach – was when he had threatened to *get* one of the girls for cutting him off after nine beer. After he said it to Ruby, she came and got me, and at that point he smashed a pool cue over the bar and said he was going to shove the sharp end up her cunt. He ended up hitting *me* with it, right across the face so that there was a red mark that started as a gouge near the corner of my mouth and ended in a deep purple scrape near my temple that wouldn't go away for a long time. I hit him out of pure instinct – the only guy I ever hit at the job – then I choked him out from behind, dragged his body out the door. When he woke up, in my arms, with the cops there, he was crying. Suddenly, he was the ordinary, fucked-up guy he always was.

What happened, Jimmy? he asked, looking up at me, terrified, clutching my arm. Did something happen?

I remembered the time he had noticed me reading a book before my shift and had asked what it was about. Had talked about how he'd always wanted to read books, and so I just gave it to him. When he woke up after I hit him, he had the same look on his face as when I gave him that paperback.

What happened? He was almost in tears.

And I was so disgusted with him and myself and the job all I could manage to say was *fuck you*.

Then, *it's alright, Cal*.

And then, *I don't know why any of this happened*.

Kelly knew the story, even though she wasn't there that night, and she knew who he was and *what* he was. But that day at the beach, when I came back in my boots and swim trunks, she was shaking her head at me. Her whole body was shaking, and she said that she wanted to leave.

No, I told her. We aren't leaving.

She looked at me, still shaking her head, still trembling all over, probably feeling or thinking something I couldn't possibly have understood at the time. I imagine now that she could've been seeing what we were coming to, or where we are now. She might've been seeing all the things she was stuck with, and seeing them all at once.

Later, I noticed I had blood in the hairs on my stomach and chest.

Later, I told her it couldn't have gone differently, but you could say that about most anything. So I tried saying *it couldn't have been helped* and she said no, *you couldn't help it*.

She had the same look on her face when Eddie and I are in the hospital, getting put back together. When she looks at me and says the same thing as the city council guys. Asks *what were you even doing there?*

I had nothing to say to that one at all, just like I had nothing to say to her on the beach. The difference is maybe that I can see she's right this time. With that, a thought that starts as a secret forms in me and gets bigger and bigger until it takes up all the sky in my head. The thought hangs over everything, and is something everyone probably already knows about me. The idea's pretty simple. That there's something in me that ought not to be there.

∞

When my hero, Tom Stone gets out of the hospital, he spends all his time downstairs in his pajamas, staying warm by the wood stove. He looks like hell, his cheeks grey and unshaven, big rings under his eyes, but still looks better than he did in his hospital room.

They didn't find evidence of a heart attack, heart disease, or stroke. It wasn't low blood sugar, or diabetes or the rare stuff like those thyroid conditions or Addison's disease. His blood pressure *was* through the roof when they took him in, but since then it's been normal and steady. Stress. Stress was the final diagnosis.

Now I'm on fucking pills that they don't even know if I need, he says. He looks angry, angry enough that I'm actually thinking about his blood pressure, watching red rise on his cheeks like when Donald Duck gets really pissed. I wonder for the first time – do I sound like that?

Then he launches into one of those speeches you hear from guys that almost died. About how everything's in perspective now, and how he needs to get everything in order while he still can. About how he knows what's important, and what the right thing to do is. There's something so desperate in his eyes and his mouth is strained, like it's hard to say the words, so I say *whatever you need, Tom,* and he grabs my knee so hard it feels like he's going to snap it off like a beer cap.

Once he finally gets down to it, he also says it's important that I don't ask questions about what he's going to get me to do, and asks that I keep it to myself.

You know, he says. As one man to another.

Sure.

It's all just a mess, you know? You can make a mess no matter what you do, he says.

I think I know what he's saying, and the way he's looking at me, it's like he knows I know.

It's time to make a change, he says. Time to get things all lined up.

OK.

Things can be a real mess if you just let them go on their own, he says.

OK.

Next, I'm driving his half-ton through the snow with an envelope he gave me, an envelope that I know is full of cash the moment I touch it. There's a house, I'm told, a little house – it's on the run, in the next county – mint green with a red door. If I could drop off that package, it would mean an awful lot. Make sure to ask for Gene, I'm told. The house he collapsed in front of is nearby. He was either coming from, or going to this house in particular.

No one answers the door. I knock on it for a long time before I notice a doorbell and no one comes when I press that either. Eventually I see a white face in the big living room window. It's startling, because the face is so low in the window that I get the feeling they must be crouching or lying down. Hiding. She's her mid-50s maybe, blonde with a saggy face, staring at me from behind a big house plant, condensation building and shrinking around her mouth. Where her sobs are coming in and out. She keeps saying something, but I don't know what it is. Says it as many times as she exhales, until I can't see her through the little pane anymore.

Somewhere in the distance, I hear all the times I said crap about Tom being the kind of man I admired, or the kind of father I wished I had. Him and me on the couch with a couple beer, rolling our eyes at Kelly and saying *women*. The look on Kelly's face when she stares my way.

Then there's the Christmases where Kelly and I don't go home – where we spend money we don't have and go to Whistler instead, and the one after that where we stay in to celebrate, just us.

The anniversary in our hotel room, where she gets mad at me – screaming mad – for joking about my non-existent mistress, as if she were waiting in the other room to meet her.

This Christmas just past, where her and Tom hug for so long that it's awkward for everyone in the room. When they pull away, both their eyes have that glassy, near-tears look, and it occurs to me that it *has* been a long time since we've seen Tom.

Her mother, who never says or does anything beyond looking out the window and smoking cigarettes, who speaks in a voice so quiet it's like she says no regular sentences, only secret ones. Those deep purple bags under her eyes.

Later, I get the idea, watching Kelly clean her father's house, that maybe you can throw yourself into something hard enough that you can cancel out all of your other problems. I watch her scrub the baseboards, scrub them white, and I can see how hard Tom would work, pushing himself to the point of exhaustion, all day, every day, until he just shut off, out in the middle of nowhere. All the things that move him forward no longer firing.

∞

I go back to Ron's, re-apply to my old job. I'm told, with tenderness, that it's already been filled, despite being promised it was mine whenever I wanted it back. Maybe because he knows I show up on time and will at least keep the bar safe, or maybe just because he feels guilty, Ron offers me a spot as the day bartender, two or three shifts a week. I take it, and have to endure being trained by a girl half my age, at a place I've worked at for so long it feels like my living room.

I think about the grey, wet streets back in Sudbury county, and the rich, corporate fucks and punks they got going around in huge green trucks marked TRIUS these days. I think about the way they would look coming up the road to the Clifton farm, the way the truck would shine in the daylight, and what it would look like from their trash-scattered yard.

Their family is on my mind a lot, sort of placed on a balance beam with me and mine on the other side so I can draw comparisons and make promises to myself. I dream about them, dream about old West standoffs where I have to keep them out of the bar, destroy their whole posse before they spread and run us over, before they surge over the hills and multiply.

I dream about Tom, Tom's wives, Tom's daughters. The thing that everyone used to say about us – *you're just like him* – just keeps on sounding in my head again and again, and suddenly it's like all I'm a woman who's realized she's gotten fat, looking in the mirror, sucking in her cheeks, looking again and again in different poses like maybe it'll go away if you see from just the right angle.

During the daytime, I find myself searching through the paper for the most fucked-up story while my five or six regulars sit and drink. They know me as the Guy Who Threw People Out, so they hold me in some kind of reverence, and don't mind that I don't refresh their drinks as much as I should or give them the right change. I always look for that one screwed-up, horrible story so I can read it out loud and hear those magic words: *the world's going to hell*, or *what's wrong with people*, or *what a whack-job*. I want to hear it from people who are turning their paycheck into beer, or putting the whole thing into some machine with flashing lights that just swallows it all up and keeps swallowing. I want to hear someone I've had to kick out for drawing on the walls ask *why would someone go and do something like that?* I want to hear it so I can lean in and look into their eyes and see if anything's happening in there, see if they're even thinking about the question they just asked. Find out if it's just something they said because they're supposed to.

After doing that, I probably turn and do something automatically, something I don't even think about or register as a choice in my brain, something I would barely remember a moment later like when I touch the pile of ice in the sink with my whole hand, or imagine the people in the beer posters coming to life and walking around and saying stuff to me that sometimes makes sense and sometimes means nothing.

My new hours almost match up with Kelly's perfectly and I end up spending most of my week with her, bothering her while she's reading or just following her around the house. I lie on the couch and watch her a lot, and further cement my body and brain's decisions about her.

One time when she's trying to make supper, I keep getting in her way until she just tells me to sit down at the dinner table. She feeds me little pieces of bread and cheese and fruit and whatever she's using to make supper and I have one of those moments, those surges of love for her that's stronger than ever. I get another one of those big, uncontrollable hard-ons, and she says *what* because of how I'm looking at her.

I love her so much I squeeze and crack the glass of juice she gave me and my hand even starts to bleed.

Did you just break that glass? She asks.

I tell her yeah, and I hold it in my hand, nice and tight so the red blooms against the glass:

I love you.

Martha Bátiz

THE LAST CONFESSION

My name is Marcela, but I'm still startled when someone calls out the name "Maria." I shiver, I have this urge to run away as fast as I can… My heart beats, my hands sweat… It's absurd, especially in the middle of winter. Here, freezing wind is the only enemy. It hurts to breathe, but I know there are worse things. The wind reminds me I am in Toronto and no matter how much I miss the warmth of the sun all year round, and the mangoes that grow in the tree in my mother's backyard, I'm safe. But for how long? I had just come out of the shower this morning when I turned on the radio and heard the news. The government back home has been overthrown. Political prisoners are being freed. Trials will be held. I had dreamed about this moment – how I'd react, what I might say. In spite of it all, I had envisioned receiving the news while in the company of my loved ones, never alone like this. I had expected to feel overjoyed. But I peed in my underwear. After cleaning myself, I didn't know what else to do, so I phoned Farah:

"Congratulations! You must be elated!" she said, as soon as she recognized my voice.

I took a deep breath. It was hard to find air to push the words out.

"Can I see you, please? I need to talk."

"What about the snowstorm? They say it will be big this time."

This Canadian habit, this talking about the weather all the time, drives me crazy. Farah, of all people, should know there are more urgent, grave matters to worry about.

"The forecast people always exaggerate. Please, Farah. I'm begging you."

She agreed to meet me at the café close to her apartment building. I have time to get everything ready. The bed is unmade, the bookshelf is half-empty, and I still have yesterday's coffee ageing on the stove. I take a piece of paper, a pen I brought home from work and sit down, close my eyes and see Tomás' face, his fat-framed glasses, and the freckles on his nose. He was very serious and committed, but also had the most contagious laughter. I write down *Tomás*, and a knot takes my throat hostage. I need a few moments to be able to breathe again, to focus again, and write down his last name. I can't go on. I have to stop. I get up and walk towards the window. I hesitate before lifting the corner of the curtain to look outside. My knees are trembling, but my back is covered in sweat, so I know it's not the old heater's fault this time.

Maybe I should have chosen a different name, but Maria seemed just right: back then I, too, was a virgin. The control I had over my body made me feel strong. Maria was the name I used for our work underground. I thought I would be protected by its profound religious meaning, but also because it is such a common name. I was wrong. When they arrested me they knew exactly who I was. They knew Marcela, and they knew Maria, and nothing could save me.

This is my second winter in Toronto. I tell myself I like winter because it helps me to stay focused on the present. I peek out under the curtain and see the sky is white. I can't make out a single cloud. I hope the storm is a tough one. The sun that smiled at me from the blue sky during the summer was an injection of melancholy: I got homesick. That's why I have been doing the opposite of what everybody else normally does around here: I go out and take long walks when it is grey and snowing, but when it is hot I try to stay indoors as much as I can. In the beginning I left the curtains and the windows shut, but memories of the time when I didn't know whether it was day or night, or if it had rained, were too strong. I opted to stay indoors, curtains closed but windows wide open. The breeze pushed sunshine my way; allowing the light back in was a little victory. I live on the sixth floor. Nobody was spying on me from the outside. I kept reminding myself that this was Toronto, but the heat and the humidity somehow fooled me. I couldn't stop thinking of my last days back home. During winter I'm more at ease. When it's snowing I don't have to be so vigilant. The scarf over my face helps me feel protected. The crispy – or slushy - sounds beneath my boots let me know if I am alone. I know immediately when someone is behind me; I seek refuge against a wall and let the person – or persons – pass, and then keep walking.

I met Farah at work, Aunt Clara. We are telemarketers. It's not a nice job, but it is the only one I could get as a newcomer, and it helps me pay my rent and food. I walk to the office, sit down at my little desk, and tackle faceless names and numbers they assign to me. I call the customers and read my script to them and most of the time they hang up on me or insult me or yell at me, how dare I interrupt their meal or their work or their privacy or whatever. At the beginning I couldn't sell anything, so one morning my boss threatened to fire me, which then turned out to be a blessing because that's how Farah and I became friends. I was crying in the washroom during one of our breaks. She offered me some advice. She gave me a hug! Nobody had touched me since I'd left home. I just broke down when I felt her warmth, her smell of saffron and sandalwood. I hugged her back and thought I would never be able to stop crying. She later joked that I had made her *chador* all wet, and I asked her what a *chador* was, and when she told me we both smiled.

Our office is a small place, yet everyone comes from a different country (none from mine, though, and nobody speaks Spanish except me). If somebody took a picture of my coworkers and myself together, and sent it back home, my cousins would laugh and say we look like one of those old ads that *Benetton* posted everywhere in the eighties. Yes, in my country we were never rich but we were trendy and aware of the latest fashions, even if the faces on the poster didn't resemble our daily world. Ours is a homogenous society, that's why we were so easy to catch, so easy to brainwash. But I like to fantasize: with such a picture in my hand, I would tell my family something like this: "*sí*, in Toronto I don't even know where in the map to find the country where this coworker here comes from, but that's okay because we smile at one another every morning and sometimes we share food, and it's a great feeling, *sabes?*" My cousin Pedro would have known what I mean. Not only would he have understood, he'd have wanted to come and see for himself. Maybe even try to hook up with some girl whose name he would have fun mispronouncing... *Ay, Pedro*, I miss you so much. If we only knew where your body is, what they did to you... My Aunt Clara has probably worn herself out by now looking for him, trying to find anything out, her hair had already turned grey when they arrested me, and she was not even fifty. If only I was brave enough to speak with her again…

I'm happy – if you can ever be happy about things like these – that my mom wasn't alive when they took me. I couldn't have handled the thought of them doing something to her because of me. I couldn't have handled the thought of her crying because of my choices. And if somebody had ever told me that the only person who would have understood me was the woman underneath the black veil, I wouldn't have believed it. But now I live in Toronto, and since I take walks at 30 degrees below zero, anything is possible.

Farah, a few years older than me, has the most beautiful dark hair. I saw it when she took off her veil – we were alone – to show me her biggest scar. In both our countries, anyone who is against the regime gets killed. Or imprisoned and tortured, at least in mine until this morning. Farah and I have a lot in common: we know what pain and fear taste like, the flavor and texture of our blood. We both have lost everything and everyone. Other people's cries are like tattoos inside my skull. Shrill, deep, under a tsunami of loud *salsa* music. I have nightmares almost every night: I deserve them. That's why I won't ever be able to face Aunt Clara and my cousins again. That's why I'm glad my mother passed away before all this happened.

I need to go back to the letters, back to writing the list, but it's so hard. It's much nicer to just stand here by the window. The streets are almost empty, which is strange considering it's Saturday, and the storm is scheduled to begin later this afternoon. I can't help smiling when I see someone walking their dog and the dog is all dressed up. If Aunt Clara had heard about dogs wearing boots, she would have laughed until her jaws hurt. Some dogs' boots are nicer and cozier than mine. Farah thinks it's funny, too. She belongs to a group of survivors and refugees who get together every once in a while to comfort one another. She has asked me to come along, but I don't know if I can do that. I don't know if I can endure listening to their stories. And I would be so scared to find someone from my homeland, what would I say then? What excuse could I give? How could I ever look them in the eye? With Farah it's different. We can laugh at dogs wearing matching boots and coats, and if we feel like it, we can also talk, but mostly we don't anymore, and that's fine. She doesn't know my entire truth. Nobody does. The moment my words have a sound of their own and leave my body they will be impossible to take back. And I'm scared to confront them. In English there is a word or a name for almost everything. *Refugee*, or *PTSD* are some of the first I learned. When they are said out loud, people seem to understand, they turn benevolent and generous. Nothing wrong with that, but what do they really understand, I wonder? Unlike me, most of them do know where their loved ones have been laid to rest.

There is another convenient word to go with this, too, which I was taught upon arrival: *closure*. What an unbearable, cruel word. A pain so big can't be closed down.

Many times I've wondered about what Aunt Clara would say if I told her that people in Toronto actually *live* in basements. And that, when I refused to rent one, all I had to say was, "I'm a refugee and have been diagnosed with PTSD, so I can't live in a basement, thank you." Very polite, very politically correct. I am a fast learner. Nobody needs to know what happened – or if anything happened at all. Aunt Clara would have understood, though. She too would have rejected the basement apartment.

I got sick at work once. There was a mouse underneath one of the desks, a little brown mouse. I screamed so loudly I scared everyone. I ran to the washroom and locked myself in; I felt like my heart was about to break free from my chest. I threw up all over my clothes, and was practically out of breath when the paramedics arrived. There's a name for that, too: *panic attack*. Farah looked me in the eye, she knew there were no words to describe what had driven me to the washroom. "Whenever you're ready," she'd said, "I'll be there." Hence today's call, the letters and the list. I will take her at her word. Our English is equally awkward, but I have learned since I arrived in Toronto that all languages become the same when spoken through sorrow.

I go back to the table and write *Rosa*. A chubby girl, with curly hair and incredibly white teeth; an only child. She lived with her dad, an old-fashioned man who wanted her to get married and have many children. She'd have none of that, Rosa... In English there are so many names and words for everything, but back home and in those days we used mostly one: *mierda*. Instead of saying, "the regime is corrupt," we would say, "*el régimen es una mierda.*" Instead of saying, "we need to solve this problem," we said "*debemos resolver esta mierda.*" And of course, instead of saying someone had been "traumatized," we said "*lo hicieron mierda;*" they turned him to shit. And so, as I work down the list, and begin to write the letters, with every word I shape I tremble, I fight the urge to cry, I must not cry. By the time I'm finished I know I have to leave to meet Farah. It's so hard, however, to get up, put on my coat and my scarf and mittens and boots. I feel weak, scared; what if I don't go? I can call her and cancel. The storm would be a good excuse, she'd understand. But when I look at the envelopes I have in my hand, I know I must go. I don't want to bundle up, though. A sweater should do. I fold the documents, put them in my pocket, take my keys and leave without looking back.

The cold is numbing, yet, on this frigid noon, as I walk through the snow, I feel surprisingly alert. I give myself strength by remembering Farah's laughter when I told her how Pedro and I would climb the mango tree in my mother's backyard and make a mess of our clothes eating all the mangoes, sitting there on a branch; and how my mother and Aunt Clara smiled at us and said we were the most beautiful monkeys they had ever seen. She had similar stories from back home, near the Caspian Sea, but they used to eat dates over there. So one day she brought in dates and I brought in some sliced mangos and we shared our lunch quietly; we never did that again because we felt so sad. We decided tuna sandwiches are easier to share – no memories for either of us. Aunt Clara would have said we were silly girls, and perhaps she would have been right. What will she think when she learns that in this woman from another faith and another language and another part of the world I have found not just my only friend, but the solution to my plight? Maybe getting to know her was why destiny brought me to live here.

January is a good time for new beginnings. Back home it's summer, and history is being written, as they said on the radio. Except I don't think they know, those Canadian radio hosts, that history is usually not written down in my country without first being beaten into the people. I wonder what is truly going on, but don't really want to find out. As I approach the café where I am to meet Farah, I think of Aunt Clara. She used to say that hope and calm always come together. I think she must have been wrong, because even though I have found hope, I am not calm. I'm shivering and my teeth are chattering and on the way here some peo-ple stared at me like I come from another planet. One woman even offered me her scarf. Why would I want a stranger's scarf? What difference would it make?

As I walk, I can't help but think of how I put my story into words for Farah to read. I cannot fight any-more and begin to cry, and the cold air mocks me and threatens to freeze my eyes but I don't care. There were five of them around me, soldiers, laughing. They were new; I had never heard their voices before. I was tied up to the smelly, sticky operating table where they used to bring us in for questioning. The whole room stank of blood and sweat and mold. It was humid and cold and echoey, like basements usually are. The soldiers stank of cheap cologne. I always felt the urge to vomit when they brought me in, but how many times can you vomit on an empty stomach? I was expecting electric shock, a beating, or being raped again. I never knew what would come first, my entire body was on alert. All of a sudden, I felt something cool and heavy on my stomach. They informed me it was a small, metal cage. I heard a slight screech and then felt some cool paws and tiny claws scratching my skin. What is this, I asked, not daring to move. They removed my blindfold and the light hurt my eyes. After a few moments, I saw it: a big, black rat on top of my naked chest. It was sniffling, exploring me. I tried not to breathe. I didn't want it to bite me. The soldiers laughed and put minced meat on my breast, just a handful. It felt cold and wet. One of the soldiers said that the rat hadn't had anything to eat for days. My body was shaking against my will, and even though I was holding my lips closed tight I must have scared the rat because I felt its teeth pinching my skin. I started to scream and squirm. The rat scratched me before falling on the floor. The men were pissed off. They had to catch the rat again and they didn't like that, so one of them hit me while another put the blindfold back on. Once they caught the rat one of them said he felt like masturbating: it was a pity the rat was going to have me, and not him. "You can squirm all you want, cunt, but this little rodent wants his mamma." I was crying, pleading for mercy, please, let me go, please, I'll do anything, please. Another said it would be worse once they forced the animal inside my body. "Rats get scared and sometimes they get trapped in the uterus, then there's nothing we can do." I felt someone's fingers inside my vagina: "yes, there's room enough here for that little critter for sure!" I couldn't handle it, I yelled and I promised I would tell them everything they wanted to know. All the names I knew, all the aliases, everything. Yes, we had a plan to kill the *Generalissimo*. Yes, there were many of us involved. "My breast hurts," was followed by, "Your cunt will hurt more!" and when I was done talking they punched me in the stomach, "You traitor, you make us sick!" they said, and gave me an electric shock. "Because you deserve it, you coward, you piece of rat shit."

When I woke up I wasn't in my cell, but in a convent. I have no idea how I got there. And will probably never know how or why either. I didn't ask questions, and neither did they. I know it sounds strange, Farah, but it's true: the nuns helped me get out of the country and start a new life. How involved with the regime were they? Who knows? Thanks to them and the good people in a Toronto parish, where I only went to mass once, I came to this land of new beginnings and second chances. I don't think God exists. If he did, he wouldn't have created rats, or people who are willing to put rats up a woman's vagina, or people like me, who rat out their friends and family. No, I didn't want to call anyone, or see anyone before leaving. How could I? Forgive me, my dear Pedro. I was no match for you. Forgive me, Aunt Clara; I caused you more suffering when you already had enough. And please do forgive me, *mami*, for bringing such shame to our family. Tomás, Rosa, Liliana, Ismael, José, Blanca; Tomás, Rosa, Liliana, Ismael, José, Blanca; forgive me for what it is they did to you because of me. I say your names over and over again: they are my litany, almost a prayer. Only those whose names have been spoken can exist.

I'm crying so hard when I come to the café that I can't say anything to Farah. I just reach for the papers in my pocket, and give them to her. She wants to hug me, is shocked, tries to hold me back but I don't let her. People are staring. Who cares? I need to leave. If I'm numb enough from the cold it won't hurt. It will be brief. Fast. I run until she can't see me anymore. Tomás, Rosa, Liliana, Ismael, José, Blanca. It hurts to breathe even more than before, I force your names out into the icy-cold air – I can't run anymore, I'm so tired. I have the packages of powder from the hardware store in my pocket, the warfarin, I know what I must do, how I will finally break us all free, saying my name over and over again, Marcela, Marcela, Marcela, my prayer, before I became Maria.

Seán Virgo

GRAMARYE

Honesty bloomed in the witch's garden, and thrift stitched its way through the stone path to her door.

She came with the snowdrops, and left with the swallows, but a woodpile of birch and wild apple was stacked by the gate and smoke rose from her chimney all summer long.

She sat reading by the hearth while the afternoon sunlight crept in across the room towards her chair. A yellow bird sang in its cage by the window, and her cat stared out through the glass at the willow tree that shielded the house from the lane.

There was a girl staring back through the leaves. She had come with her cousin on a dare, and now they were spies, looking over the wall and into the witch's home.

The cat yawned and the witch looked up from her book. Her lips were moving.

"Do you think she can see us?" the girl whispered. "It looks like she's talking to us."

"Or singing," said her cousin. "She's casting a spell on us!" And they cycled madly back to the village, laughing in make-believe terror.

The girl's uncle cut wood for the witch, and raked her leaves in the fall. He kept an eye on her place in the winter months, too, and laughed at the stories. "There's nothing strange about her," he said. "She keeps to herself is all. No harm in that. She knows flowers better than anyone."

But "Oh," said the aunt, "you're in deep trouble now, my girl. She'll have hexed you for sure. One of these days you may find yourself growing a tail." And each time the girl walked by, her aunt would glance down, as if she were looking for signs of that sprouting tail. The girl's mother took it up too. It was all a great joke.

But the young people knew better.

There were the five who'd gone down to skate on the long pond and had stopped at the witch's house. They pelted it with snowballs, and broke a window, and within the hour felt the ice crack under them, just as the window had cracked. Two boys and a girl fell through, out of sight, and the merest miracle carried them all to the open patch of water above the weir.

The teenager who worked each Saturday in the general store told how she'd pulled a rude face at the witch's back, forgetting the mirror on the wall between the shelves. The witch had just smiled at her, but that night, as her boyfriend was driving her home from a party, a black dog ran out in front of them and they went off the road at the bend above the old quarry. The car had hung teetering on the edge of the cliff, and they sat there for hours, not daring to move, until someone drove by in the morning and sent for help.

And there was the teacher's son who fired two stones from his slingshot at the witch's cat, where it sunned itself on her steps. The witch had come out, and pointed her finger at him without a word, and on his way home the ambulance had sped by, taking his little sister to the hospital. She lay between life and death, at death's door they said, for almost a week before she awoke from her coma.

There were other stories too. It seemed to the girl that the witch was the most interesting thing about the backwater town.

They'd come down from the city to help look after her grandma. The old lady was dying, and worse than that, they said she was losing her mind. The stroke she had suffered at Christmas had stolen most of her words, and she passed the days now in her grey wing chair by the window. Sometimes, when the family was gathered and talking, her eyes became bright and watchful, even gleaming with laughter or mockery, but most of the time they stared out with intense concentration at nothing at all.

The girl was not afraid of the physical things, the nodding and throat clearing, the smells sometimes, the shawl-twitching fingers, the webs of drool to be wiped from the tremoring chin; it was the vanishing of her grandmother, the strong, humorous woman full of stories. They had always felt like conspirators, sharing a language that had skipped a whole generation. Now she could not bear to look into the faded brown eyes which all too often seemed to be gazing right through her.

Instead, she went off with her every day, pushing the wheelchair along the riverside path out of town. Walking behind, she could pretend that her grandma's eyes were alert as her own and she talked to her as though nothing had changed. But really, it was a way to be alone. At home she had taken for granted the hours she could spend with herself, but here in her aunt's house, and sharing her cousin's bedroom, there was always someone else.

Each day she walked further, turning off down the overgrown towpath that her cousin had showed her, guiding the wheelchair over ruts and between the young bushes. It was better than being alone, because thinking out loud made things clearer. She would be a teenager in just a few weeks and she had many opinions. She had questions, too, even secrets she'd kept from herself until now. The grandmother listened, and sometimes her answers came in the girl's own voice.

Across the fields you could see the big weeping willow where the cousins had spied. The thought of it cast a spell, and the witch found her way into their conversation.

"Did you know her, Grandma? You must have. Do you remember when she first arrived?"

They stopped by the ruined lock, above the dried-up canal, with their backs to the town.

"How old would you say she is? And where does she go in the winter? Where did she come from? What brought her here in the first place?"

The questions hung in the air and as no one had told her, and she couldn't have guessed, that the witch's house had once belonged to her grandmother, the girl began a story of her own as they started back towards home.

"Well, suppose she was someone's dark secret and they gave her away to the Gypsies, or the Indians, or maybe she was left by the wayside and found, yes, and she grew up speaking the language of birds and trees and stones, and then one day when she was thirteen they gave her her mother's ring and a purse with some gold coins, or a locket with a lock of hair – no, she found them hidden in a doeskin pouch behind the stairs and it wasn't a lock of hair, of course, it was a picture of her young mother, no, no – actually I bet the picture was of a house by a path through the woods they'd passed once in their wanderings, so she ventures forth, and gets lost, naturally, but with help from an owl that she rescues from a snare she comes out in a clearing, and there is the house from the picture, and she goes and knocks on the door, and—"

The wheelchair lurched against a stone, and her grandma cried out, "Ha!" as though she had been jolted out of sleep.

"Are you alright, Grandma?"

But her grandmother's eyes were smiling at her, and the pale lips trembled in a effort to speak.

The girl leaned closer, their faces almost touching, and she heard the faint words, "*Always listening.*"

"Oh I *knew* you were, Grandma," she said, though she hadn't truly believed until now that it might be so.

The old eyes called her back. She leaned closer again. "*Finish story,*" she heard.

She kissed the smooth forehead. "I'll try," she said, and tucked in the rug around the child-like legs before she set off again.

"Well, for half the year she has to go back into the wilderness or she'll lose, or maybe she already can't understand the wild things and the stones anymore, their language is fading, no, no because you see her father was really a Gypsy, or an Indian, and so... and so... "

Make-believe had always been part of their language. Her grandma was known for her brisk, no-nonsense views, her impatience with sentimentality, yet she treated some imaginary things as quite matters of fact. There were guardian angels, and spirits of hedgerows and fords, and she paid close attention to her dreams, the Wednesday night ones in particular.

There was a bookcase in her house, on the landing, that was reserved for what she called *Gramarye*. For a long time the girl thought she was saying "*Grandma read.*" It was in fairy tales that their love for each other had begun.

"But suppose, Grandma, that the father was an Elfin Knight, or perhaps he was the *grandfather*, and the witch is the child of the lost girl instead – oh..."

Her birthday gift each year since she was born had been a book of stories. There were twelve of them, each named for a colour and some of them faded and worn, and each year the gap in the *Gramarye* bookcase had grown wider. The banknotes tucked into the books had changed colour too since the year she turned seven, from brown to blue to purple to green, more generous each time.

The *Lilac Fairy Book* had come last year, and her grandma had written on the fly leaf, in her blue-black ink: *This is the last one. You will be a young woman soon, but don't forget.* The crisp enclosed bill had been rose-red, with a fierce snowy owl staring out from the frozen tundra. It was more money than she had ever held in her life.

Above Grandma's inscription were her own grand-mother's words, and in two of the books, the *Blue* and the *Red*, there were faded birthday blessings from two even earlier grandmas. It seemed to the girl that these gifts reached back almost forever.

The witch belonged, irresistibly, to the world of those books. She was hardly ever in town, the store owner delivered her groceries, and she never had visitors. The girl had caught that glimpse of her through the leaves, but each night, when they'd turned off their bedside lamps, the willow tree across the fields, and the cat in the big bay window, stole into her thoughts, maybe into her dreams.

"She has a cat and a bird, and all manner of flowers in her garden, and a fire in midsummer. I think I shall go and visit her. Do you think I should, Grandma? She has no friends, though perhaps she doesn't want any of course. But if I mean her no harm, and tell no one I've been there, what harm could she wish me? Do you think I should go?"

As the wheelchair trundled across the iron bridge into town, she took the old lady's nodding as total agreement.

She went off on her bicycle the next afternoon, the way that her cousin had showed her. "You've got such a nerve," she told herself, as others had told her before, but when she turned up the lane and the willow came closer, she began to lose heart. "I'll see if she's out in her garden," she said. "That will be a sign. If she isn't there, I'll forget it."

But the witch was there. She was kneeling at a flower bed, close to the gate, in floppy green hat and gardening gloves. She looked younger than the girl had expected.

"And what can I do for you?"

The eyes were hazel, watchful but amused. It was a kind face, apart from the scarred, twisted lips.

"I don't believe in witches."

The witch sat back on her heels. "No, I don't suppose you do," she said. "What *do* you believe in?"

The girl felt herself flushing to the roots of her hair. "I'm sorry," she said. "That was rude of me wasn't it?"

"Not rude," said the witch, and she started to pull of her gloves, "but very direct. And you haven't answered my question." Her voice was low, and gentler than her words.

"I don't think I know how to," the girl said. "I'm sorry."

"Two *I'm sorries* are quite enough for one afternoon," the witch said, and got to her feet. Her loose smock had open pockets across the front; it was the same faded green as her hat. "You'd better come in for tea, and think about it."

"All right," the girl said.

The witch's crooked smile woke a host of fine lines around her eyes. It was impossible to guess how old she might be. "You don't stay abashed for long, do you?" she said. And she came and unlatched the gate. She was a slight woman, not much taller than the girl, and though her hair was streaked with a silvery grey, it was tied back in what was almost a ponytail.

The girl followed her up the path where low pink flowers bristled between the flagstones.

The witch turned, with her hand on the doorknob.

"What's your name?"

"Melissande."

"No it isn't."

"Well, it will be one day, when I can choose."

"Fair enough," said the witch. "There's no need for names here anyway." She held the door open, and the girl stepped into a kitchen where strings of onions and garlic hung by a window, and the air smelled of herbs and lemons.

"Oh wow," she whispered. She spun around on the blue-tiled floor, taking in the pinewood dressers, the copper pans hanging above the stove, the calm, uncluttered space around the plain, heavy table.

Through the next door the living room was full of light. There were gay rugs like islands on the pale wooden floor.

"It's so much bigger and brighter than it looks from outside," the girl said. "You must love it."

The witch put her hat and gloves on the bare wooden table, and filled a kettle at the sink.

"Go and look around," she said. "I'll come through with the tea when it's ready."

The girl slipped out of her sneakers and stepped barefoot into the room. The bay window was like a room of its own, with big cushions on the floor beneath it. The cat sat on the window seat with its back to her, looking out. And there was another window, to her right, and beside that a black writing desk with elegant legs, and a painting above it of an old house among windswept trees, with low rocks in the foreground.

Across the room a staircase went up, forming a partial wall beside the fireplace. This was the space that felt the most lived in. The hearth was of grey flagstones, like those on the path outside, and a big rocking chair faced the fire, with a table beside it, a lamp and a pile of books.

It was strange how fire drew you, even on a hot July day. The girl went to it, spreading her hands as if to warm them. Two logs burned lazily on an iron cradle, and there were more logs in a basket, waiting. On the other side of the fireplace was a rush-seated stool and – oh, a real witch's broom.

She took the broom and sat on the stool, with the rough twigs between her feet, and leaned her cheek against her hands where they held the broomstick.

A fire was like water under a bridge – you could stare for hours, and almost not have to think.

She leapt up. The witch was standing at the kitchen door, with a cup in each hand, watching her.

The girl held out the broom. "Is this your midnight steed?"

For a second, the witch's eyes were like stones. Then she laughed. It was a young laugh, girlish and full of amusement. "Oh yes," she said. "Over the rooftops and under the stars, peering in windows, pilfering dreams."

The girl's cheeks were burning. "That was bold of me, wasn't it?"

The witch laughed again. "Bold? That must be your mother's word for you." She held out one of the cups. "Here, try this if you dare."

She had taken off her smock. Her skin was pale, below her neck, and a green stone hung there on an almost-invisible chain.

The cup was white and delicate; the girl could see the tea's shadow through it. The steam smelled musky, but the first sip was like rainwater might taste if you drank it out of a lily.

"What kind of tea *is* this?"

"It's *kvann* that you're smelling, angelica."

"Will it turn me into a toad?"

The witch looked at her sideways: "More likely a barn owl, don't you think?"

The girl's eyes widened. The barn owl was her special bird. She had a poster of it at home, over her bed, staring with its white heart-face from a castle window.

She went and leaned the broom against the chimney breast. On the mantel, at eye level, was a cluster of treasures just like her altar of "foundlings," as her mother called them, on the bedroom dresser at home. A banded snail shell, an ivory ring, curious stones and weathered pieces of wood. A bird's skull, a red and grey feather, a speckled sea shell with a flesh-pink cavity. And one stone that seemed to have raised white flowers all over it. She sipped the sweet tea and reached out with her left hand.

"No, don't touch, please. Just look."

"I wouldn't hurt anything."

"Some things don't want to be touched – the things from the wild – my hands are the only ones that have held them."

"What can I touch, then? You didn't mind the broom."

"Anything that's made to be used – the furniture, crockery, the books. *Things men have made and breathed soft life into.* A good angel wrote that."

"I can't tell when you're serious," the girl said. "Do you believe in angels then?"

"They are never far away. You might be an angel, sometimes, you know; an angel might inhabit you for a while, without you knowing it."

"But you said a good angel."

"Ah yes," the witch sighed. "I'm afraid there are bad ones too."

The girl felt suddenly awkward.

"Can I sit in the rocking chair?"

"Certainly you may."

The girl flung her self into the big chair, and kicked with her heels. The witch pulled the stool out, a little way onto the hearth, and sat with her knees drawn up, watching. She held her cup in both hands, and when she drank, and her lips disappeared, she looked quite different. In that light her face was unlined.

For a while there was no sound but the creak of the chair and the muttering fire.

The girl stopped, and took a book from the table beside her. "*Piano Quintet in A Major*," she read. It was a musical score. She felt her usual shame about the piano lessons.

"What do you play, what instrument?"

"I have a harpsichord in my winter house. Here, I just read."

"You read the music?"

"Yes, these are my summer books."

"And you can hear it?"

"Don't you hear when you read?"

"I suppose," the girl said. "But look, you have to read five or six lines at a time. I couldn't do that."

"But you do," the witch said. Indoors, her eyes were more green than hazel. They seemed to grow as she talked. "We read sentences and paragraphs, not words. And you're seeing things as well as hearing them, aren't you? And feeling too, and often remembering and imagining, all at the same time."

"I'll have to think about that," the girl said, and looked around for something else. She pushed herself up from the chair. "Where did your bird go?"

"My bird?"

261

"The yellow bird in the cage by the window."

The witch's eyes looked into her. "I think you must have dreamed that," she said. "*A robin redbreast in a cage, Puts all heaven in a rage.*"

"Oh," said the girl. "And I thought that your cat would be black too."

"Ah no," said the witch, "he has to be grey." And she creased up her eyes and crooked her fingers and cried in a thin, cackly voice, "*I come, Greymalkin!*"

As if it had heard, the cat looked towards them and opened its mouth in a huge, slow yawn.

"Or perhaps you haven't read that yet," the witch said in her normal voice.

"You're like my grandma used to be – full of poems and sayings."

"That's what memory's for, is it not?"

The girl frowned. That didn't make sense to her. She was about to ask the cat's name, when her eye was caught by the painting across the room.

She heard the witch laugh behind her.

"What's so funny?"

"You're such a honeybee, darting from flower to flower."

"My auntie calls me a flibbertygibbet."

"That's a word with a history," the witch said. "But no, I think honeybee suits you much better."

"Anyway," said the girl, "will you tell me about this picture? Is it a real place?"

The witch set down her cup. "It's as real as you and me."

"I love stone houses. It looks very old."

"It's old and it's new. A dead friend built it for me from the stones of a derelict lighthouse."

"Have you many dead friends?"

The witch's eyes did not leave the painting. "Oh yes," she said softly. "Have you?"

"Just my dad. And soon my grandma I suppose."

She moved back a step. "Where I'm standing, would I be on the seashore?"

"Not quite, no. You're by the grey boulder where I love to sit." The witch came and stood beside her. "The sea pinks grow here and all along the clifftops. Behind us there's a goat path going down to the cove."

"Are there goats?"

"They like to browse on the seaweed. And out in the cove there's a flat rock, you can almost walk to it at low tide, and sometimes the seals come and bask there in the sun."

"Seals."

"You can hear them on calm nights, slapping their tails and calling."

"Mermaids," the girl whispered.

"I like to think so."

There was a thud on the floor behind them. The cat was strolling towards the staircase, its tail erect and curled at the tip.

"When I look out from my work room window," the witch said, "I can see across the straits to the islands. And downstairs I have a painting of *this* house, so I won't forget."

"I've never been to the sea," the girl said. "Except when I was a baby, too young to remember."

"You'll grow accustomed to it. And you'll miss it when you're away. It calls to you in your dreams. You'll wake up wondering why everything is so quiet."

The girl had never met anyone who looked you so much in the eyes.

There was another thud. The cat had leaped up three stairs and was stretched out there, flexing his paws with another great yawn. The girl went over.

"Will he let me pet him?"

"Let him come in his own good time."

There was a window on the landing where the staircase turned back on itself. A tree was pressing its leaves against the glass.

"What's up there?"

"Up there is upstairs."

The girl set her foot on the first stair. "Am I allowed to look?"

"Yes, if you wish." The witch came and leaned on the bannister. In a mock whisper she said:

"But as she passed, they cried 'Beware
The wicked turning of the stair.'"

"I don't know that story," the girl said.

"Perhaps it's waiting for you to write it."

Their faces were close enough that the girl could smell lavender. The witch's eyes were as young and clear as her own. She might have been beautiful once, if it weren't for those poor lips.

"How old are you?"

"What did your grandmother say, the first time you asked her that?"

"*As old as my tongue and a wee bit older than my teeth.*"

"And there's no better answer."

"But how do you know that I asked her?"

"Well, what child doesn't?"

"I *would* like to write books someday," the girl confided.

"I expect you will, too. But are you going to find out the rest of the story or not?"

"Yes I am," said the girl, "*Beware, beware!*" and ran laughing, past the cat, up to the landing.

There were little pears among the leaves at the window, green and brown, almost within reach. There was a low table, too, with another altar of treasures, and against the wall beside her—

"What's this?"

The witch climbed two steps towards her. "Ah, that."

It was like a cloak on a shop window mannequin, but flat, with a spindle of dark wood where the head would have been. The fabric was velvet, dark green, and silvery where the daylight caught its folds. Perhaps it was a curtain. It was fastened below the spindle with a braided red cord.

"Is it a secret?"

The witch untied her hair and shook it loose so that it lay across her shoulders. "The best secrets are the ones people wouldn't believe even if you told them."

"So can I look then?"

The witch came a step closer. "If you must and you will, then you shall and you may."

The cord felt like silk. When the girl tugged, the cloak fell open at once.

There was an oval mirror, as tall as herself. A woman in a blue dress was looking back at her.

For a moment she thought it was her aunt Nora, her father's sister, but no, she was different. The face was familiar, though, the expression—

"It's me, isn't it?"

The witch came up and sat at the edge of the landing.

"It's who you *will* be."

The girl stared. The grown-up her seemed unaware, as if she was simply watching herself in her own mirror. She did not move when the girl did.

Something rubbed against her leg, and there was the cat, in the mirror too, arching its back by the woman's foot. In the room behind them she could see the edge of a table or desk, and a window beyond, with blue sky, like the sky through the pear tree's leaves, and a curtain shifting in a breeze.

"She looks happy," the girl said.

"And that's a blessing for you."

"So it tells you the future?"

The witch got to her feet. "*Then goes backwards and forwards*," she said, and she stepped behind the girl.

The woman in the blue dress had turned away and was going towards the window. The cat followed her.

And there in the mirror stood a child, perhaps seven or eight, with short blonde hair, dressed in striped dungarees. She was staring straight ahead, crossing her eyes and poking out her tongue, trying to touch her nose. The witch's cry of laughter set the girl laughing too.

"Is that really you?" she said.

"At my age, the glass looks backwards. It's good to be reminded."

Behind the child witch, the woman was indistinct now, gazing out through the window.

"But suppose," the girl said, "I was going to die when I was still young?"

The child leaned closer, and the witch's voice whispered in the girl's ear: "In that case, sweetheart, I would never have let you come up."

She reached forward and drew the cloak closed again over the glass.

The girl looked into the witch's face. "And it never shows you just as you are?"

"You're a gem," the witch said. She took the girl's hand and drew her back to the stairs. "Yes, there are moments in your life – just one moment perhaps – when you are exactly who you are supposed to be. If you happened to look in the mirror then, that is who you would see."

The cat seemed to flow down before them. "What do you call him?" the girl asked.

"Sometimes Memory, sometimes Amnesia. Mostly, Cat."

"You're funny."

"Not scary?"

"Can't you tell?"

"Well that's good." She let go of the girl's hand. "And now it's time for you to leave and for me to get at those irises back in the earth before they dry out."

"But," said the girl, "your young self in the mirror didn't have—"

"My mouth?" A shadow passed between them. "Yes, there was an accident. But I've always believed," she said as they walked towards the kitchen, "that when bad things happen it's really the angels sparing us from something much worse."

"I think you're brilliant," the girl said.

"Brilliant *and* funny. I wonder where you picked up that silver tongue."

The witch took her smock from the table and pulled it over her head.

The girl stepped back into her sneakers. "Thanks," she said. "Thanks for trusting me."

The witch smiled as she pulled on her gardening gloves. "Believe me, dearheart, most people would just see a mirror."

"But I'd never tell anyone, ever."

The witch gave a little nod.

As they went down the path, she stooped and broke off a pink flower. "Here," she said. "A gift to you from the sea. From the cliffs above the cove." In the sunlight her eyes were hazel again. "And there I have planted honesty with seeds from this garden."

"That's a flower too?"

The witch went over by the apple tree and came back with a small, papery disk. There were flat round seeds inside it. "Fairy silver," she said. "You hide this in a corner of your garden, and see what will happen."

As the girl cycled off, she called back: "You'll see me again, you know," and imagined the witch's reply.

She pedalled back up the lane, laughing into the wind. She rode with no hands, and sang and wove till she reached the main road.

This was what glee meant.

She coasted past the towpath entrance and over the bridge. She was singing the song that she and her cousin had danced to the night before.

She was the luckiest girl alive.

The adults were wonderfully incurious about her comings and goings. They had other things on their minds, and were grateful for the time she spent with the old lady. So was her cousin. "You're great with old Nana," she said. "I find her creepy, though I know I shouldn't."

The girls had known each other all their lives. They listened to music together, and compared their breasts in the bedroom mirror, but the cousin had her own friends in town, and wanted to be with them, though the girl was not unwelcome. They would hang around the old store porch, or go off down the riverbank to the swimming hole under the white cliff.

One day as she lingered on the bridge, watching the swallows race their reflections on the water, a boy took her hand, and asked her to walk with him up to the Folly on the ridge. "I don't think I'm ready for that," she told him. "You're weird," he said, but no one was watching and he didn't seem too put out. In her mind she told him, "And you're not ready for that either, if you only knew," and looked in his eyes and saw that he did know that, actually. They smiled at each other and ran to catch up with the rest.

The next morning she had to struggle to come awake. Her cousin was dressed already, toying with her hair in the mirror. "You talk in your sleep, you know," she said.

The girl sat up in bed. "What about?"

"It's like hearing someone on the phone, like one half of a conversation."

"And what do I say?"

"Well, I'm not taking notes. I'm trying to get back to sleep."

The girl reached for her clothes. "Did I talk last night?"

"Something about *But they'll miss me* and then *But will you always be there?* She looked up in the mirror: "So, is there *someone* I don't know about?"

"Don't be a cretin. Was that all?"

"The last thing was you sat up and said *Amnesia Cat* and laughed out loud." Her cousin left the mirror and bent to put on her shoes. "I was going to throw something at you, but then you shut up, thank god."

"I wonder if someone was having the other half of my dream," the girl said.

"You're truly weird," said her cousin, and reached to pinch the girl's ribs on her way to the door.

The girl ran after her. "Bitch, perv, anarchist!" she yelled, and then shrieked and ran back into the bedroom.

She rolled on the bed in hilarious shame. Her uncle had been standing at the foot of the stairs, looking up, open-mouthed.

He wasn't there at the table when the girl came down, but each time their eyes met, the cousins broke out into helpless giggles. The women looked at each other. Her mother shook her head. "I suppose we were just as bad, heaven help us," she said.

Though the girl had forgotten her dreams, she remembered what she had decided as she'd waited for sleep.

But her grandma had had a bad night, they said. She had better stay at home. After lunch, though, they relented. "Just don't go too far," the girl's mother told her. "We have to be careful."

"I know," the girl said, but her mind was already on its way.

"It's a secret, Grandma," she said as she closed the gate. "I have a new friend, and you're going to meet her now." Her grandma did look very pale but her eyes were alive, and her head moved a little from side to side as if she was watching everything.

As they passed the towpath and headed instead up the hill, the girl said, "I wonder if you can guess." And bent to hear the old lady whisper, *"Caution."*

She laughed – it didn't mean *Be careful,* it was one of her grandma's quaint sayings. *You are a caution!* always said with a smile for her granddaughter's headstrong ways.

The hill seemed much longer today, walking and pushing, and the midsummer sun threw almost no shadow at all. By the time they turned into the lane the girl was too weary to talk. She leaned heavily on the wheelchair and went at a snail's pace.

She'd feel quite the fool if the witch wasn't home. But the witch was, of course. She came out at the back door as the gate clicked shut, and waited on the path.

"Hello, Helen," she said. "It's good to see you again." And she took a frail hand from the old lady's lap, and held it in both of hers.

"How did you know Grandma's name?"

The witch looked up, puzzled. "But your grandmother grew up in this house. I bought it from her."

"How very strange," the girl said, "that no one ever said so."

"Well, it will be happy to see her again."

The grandmother was gazing up at the witch and struggling to speak. The girl leaned forward, straining to hear her.

"She said *dear Jessica*!"

"Ah," said the witch. "Then my secret's out."

She looked very slender beside the wheelchair, almost fragile in her long, dark dress. Her hair was loose, but swept to one side by a plain silver clasp. There was an amber bracelet on her left wrist.

"You're so elegant today," the girl said. "Did you know we were coming?"

She half expected the witch to say, "Well of course."

"On a day hot as this, I felt like staying indoors and reading."

"Tchaikovsky?"

The witch tossed back her hair, with that girlish laugh. "Something less earnest than that," she said. "Let's get your grandmother out of the sun."

Between them they eased the wheelchair over the threshold. The girl pushed it through to the living room, and reached down to loosen the security strap.

"Well?" said the witch.

"I suppose you can guess why I've come."

"Did you need a reason?"

All at once the girl found herself tongue-tied. She felt tired and foolish, and she wished she could just disappear. She was saved by the cat. It came flowing down the stairs and padded across the room, straight to the wheelchair. It sniffed at the rug around the grandmother's legs and leapt up onto her lap. The old lady gave a start, and then relaxed. The cat curled itself under the pallid hands, and closed its eyes.

"Wow," the girl said.

"Wonders will never cease," said the witch.

The girl took a breath. "You see," she said, "I thought that perhaps we could show my grandma the mirror."

She looked down. The silence went on forever.

"You are an extraordinary child."

"Only I didn't know if it had to be up there at *the turning of the stair*. Because we couldn't—"

"The mountain will come to Mohammed," the witch said. "Why don't you move the wheelchair to face the fire?"

She climbed to the landing and then came slowly back down. One hand was behind the mirror, holding it upright beside her, in its green cloak. They were like two people descending the staircase together.

She set it down on the hearth, and the girl manoeuvered the wheelchair in front of it.

"Go ahead, then."

The girl tugged the red cord, and watched her grandmother's face. The old eyes, almost closed now under their blue-veined lids, were suddenly wide open and a child's voice cried, "I remember!

"Yes, I remember. It was my birthday, and they let me stay up long past my bedtime." The old lips were mouthing the words, but it was the child in the mirror, a little girl in a brown dress with a wide lace collar, who was speaking.

Behind her was a room with a high ceiling, and a long table under a chandelier, laid out as if for a dinner party. The cat was not in the mirror, and there were no other people except the young witch – though not so young as before – and the grown-up girl – who had grey hair now, and a cane – and they were fading already, transparent phantoms in the grandmother's world.

The mirror had different rules.

"They gave me posset," the mirror child said. "They brought me posset, and they all drank my health."

She laughed and turned round to look back, and the witch said, "Well, we shall make her posset then. Come into the kitchen and help me – she's happy with her own company."

But the girl could not move. There were figures moving behind the child now – women and men in long-ago clothes who glided, as if they were dancing. She could not stop looking, but she wanted to, badly. She was getting scared, scared even of the mirror child who was once her grandma. It was as though her real grandma had vanished, for the girl could not drag her eyes from the mirror. She felt as though she was fading away herself. Where was she? Perhaps she would never come back.

She felt a gentle pinch at her cheek. The witch was standing there, with a small saucepan in her hand. The grandmother was gazing into the mirror world, eyes wide, her lips moving as the child chattered on. "Come now," the witch said. "I need you to help me."

The girl followed into the kitchen. "I was frightened to death," she said.

"So I saw, "said the witch. "That's the way with a wondering heart. Now, this is the first stage."

She was pouring thick cream into the saucepan.

The girl recovered herself. "So what is this 'posset'?"

"Just watch. The wine comes next."

It was a dusty bottle, with a galleon on the label. "Madeira," the witch said, "from the Islands of the Blest."

"Are you making a potion?"

"I suppose I am."

Then, "Can you hear that?"

The witch listened. "Yes, just," she said. "It's a very strong memory."

Beneath the child's prattle there were faint voices, as though a whole gathering of people were there. And music, even fainter, like a music box playing in a faraway room.

The girl let out a big sigh. "You couldn't make this up," she said. "No one would believe you."

The witch was stirring wine into the simmering cream. "Remember what I said to you, about secrets? Now will you warm this up with hot water, please?"

It was like a child's teapot, but with handles at both sides.

"What's this?"

"That is an old posset cup. Just fill it with hot water and rinse it out."

"You have everything, don't you?" the girl said.

"Well, actually, that came with this house. It was in the back of a cupboard. Now, bring it over and watch."

The witch set the cup down on the table and slowly poured in the potion. The girl watched the thick cream float up, and then a froth that rose through it slowly, almost to the cup's brim.

"There," said the witch. "I'll carry it through. Here's a cloth for her lap, and a napkin. It's party time!"

The voices were gone as they walked through, but the mirror child was still talking "—because they said that when I was nine I might have a pony. Mother said that was much too young, but she was only teasing, and then we all laughed."

"Shoo, Cat," the witch said, and the cat leaped down with a chirruping cry. The girl laid the cloth across her grandmother's lap, and "Here you are Helen," the witch said, and "My posset," the child's voice cried.

"We'll set it down on your lap, now," the witch told her. And to the girl: "Take the spoon." It was china too, with the same swirled pattern as the cup. The old hands shook as they curled around the cup, though the hands in the mirror were steady.

"Now first," said the birthday girl, "you start with the grace." You could tell she was parroting an adult. "The grace is the foam on the top, and you mustn't eat greedily, and *never* wipe your mouth with your hand. That is what the napkin is for."

What a prim little creature she was, with her shoulder-length ringlets.

The girl wiped her grandmother's lips after every spoonful. The child in the mirror wiped her own. The witch stepped back, and stood watching by the fire.

"And then comes the custard. Remember, just a little at a time, be ladylike."

A sly look came into the grandmother's eyes.

"Then they let me take a sip from the spout, the real wine. I had such a good sleep that night."

The grandmother tilted her face towards the cup. The girl helped lift it to her lips, and when she had sipped, and a little had spilled down her chin, she let go, and sighed. Her hands lay open on her lap.

"This has been the best day of my life," the little voice said, and then the old eyes drooped, and Grandma's head fell forward into sleep.

The witch was standing by the mirror. She drew the cloak over it. "There," she said.

The girl reached for the cloth and the spoon, and stumbled against the wheelchair. The cup flew out of her hand, and smashed on the floor. Wine ran out in all directions.

She let out an anguished cry. "I'm so sorry," she sobbed. She was appalled and fearful.

The witch came and held both her shoulders. The green eyes looked into her, piercing and kind. "Nothing happens by accident," she said. "Don't worry about it. I'll clean up later."

"And oh," cried the girl, "It must be so late. They'll be wondering."

The witch helped her out through the kitchen, and came to the gate. "Goodbye, Helen," she said. "Sweet dreams, you old dear."

The girl ran back towards town, as fast as she dared, and her grandma slept on, despite all the joltings and turns.

Her uncle met them at the bridge. "They won't be too pleased," he said. "We've been looking all over."

"Oh stop fussing," the grandmother said, quite loud and distinct.

"Imagine that," said the uncle, staring down at her. "And look at you, Mother – you've got roses in your cheeks."

The girl's aunt was standing at the garden gate, her hands on her hips. She hurried forward, without looking at the girl.

"You all right, Mom?"

The old lady stared at her blankly.

"Well, no harm's done, I suppose," the aunt said. "She looks quite comfortable – though she'll need cleaning up."

Nothing more was said. That evening the girls went to a movie in the school gym. It was full of screams and murders and terrified babysitters hiding in closets. The audience was loud, and entirely young.

They walked home through the twilight.

"Can you keep a secret?" her cousin said.

"Of course I can."

"I had my first real kiss today. My whole body's on fire."

"Oh yuck," said the girl. "Who was it, that boy from the drugstore?"

"As if. You will never know."

"Then why did you tell me?"

"To drive you insane with envy."

They chased each other home under the streetlights.

The last thing her cousin said as she turned off her lamp was, "Try not to talk tonight, okay? I'd like to enjoy my own dreams, pretty please."

The girl lay awake for a long time, dispelling the stupid terrors of the movie before she could take herself back through the whole afternoon. What a secret they had, just herself and the witch and her grandma, and no one to disbelieve.

But some time in the small hours of that night the grandmother's heart stopped beating and the girl walked back in a dream where the pink flowers shivered in the wind and gulls hung beside her, wings motionless over the cove.

She stopped at the house door and looked out across to the islands. The sea wind was on her face, and a curtain billowed out from the window upstairs where a story lay waiting, unfinished, on her father's desk.

Why was everything so quiet all at once? She lay alone in the darkness.

She could hear her cousin's soft breathing across the room, and then the thin shriek of a barn owl, hunting somewhere out in the night.

She opened her eyes, and shut them again at once. The streetlight's glow through the curtains was breaking the spell. Her dream was fading out of reach.

The owl cried again, far away, and she pulled the sheet over her face. She closed her eyes tightly, shutting out every distraction and yes, there it was, the slow murmur of waves, the gulls crying. She could smell the sea, and see the islands, and the house was there as before.

And now she will open the door and go in, up the stairs, to the room with the desk and the mirror, and find out perhaps how the story will really end.

Christine Miscione of Hamilton, Ontario, has recently completed an M.A. in English Literature from Queen's University in Kingston. Her work has appeared in *This Magazine*, the *Puritan*, and *529: An Anthology*. In 2011 she received a Hamilton Arts Award for writing.

Leon Rooke is the author of seven novels, sixteen short story collections, one poetry volume, and several stage plays, among other works. Also an artist, his paintings and sculptures show at Toronto's Fran Hill Gallery. Recognitions  include a Governor General's Award (*Shakespeare's Dog*), the Canada-Australia prize, the W.O. Mitchell prize, a CBC Fiction Award, the North Carolina Literature Award, and two ReLits (poetry and short fiction). He lives in Toronto.

Kelly Watt has lived in India, Mexico, France, Canada and the U.S., but now resides in Flamborough, Ontario. She has contributed to travel, health, and medical magazines/journals, and travelled across Canada as the writer and coordinator for CBC's *Front Page Challenge*. Her award-winning short fiction has been published in the *Malahat Review, Blood and Aphorisms, SOL Literary Magazine: English Writing in Mexico*, and the anthologies *She Writes* (2002) and *Best of Canadian Short Stories* (2004). Her novel is *Mad Dog*.

Darlene Madott is a Toronto lawyer and writer. She has worked editorially for *Saturday Night* and *Toronto Life* magazines, and written book reviews for the *Globe and Mail*. She has published the collection of stories *Bottled Roses,* a

film script *Mazilli's Shoes,* and the collection *Joy, Joy, Why Do I Sing?* She has received the 2002 Paolucci Prize from the Italian American Writers' Association, the Bressani Literary Award, 2008, and has published in *Accenti* magazine, *Italian Canadian Voices, More Sweet Lemons 2,* a special Sicilian edition of *Descant* and *Bravo!*

Linda Rogers, a Canada's People's Poet for 2000, former Victoria Poet Laureate, and a winner of the inaugural Montreal Poetry Prize, is a journalist, poet, lyricist and novelist. She is the recipient of the Cardiff, Bridport and Kenney  Awards in England, the Voices Israel Prize, the Leacock, Livesay, Arc, Acorn, and National Poetry Prize awards in Canada, and the Rukeyser Award in the U.S,. among others. Rogers' recent books include *The Third Day Book* and *Raise the Homing.*

 **Daniel Perry** of Toronto has twice won fellowships in the Summer Literary Seminars Unified Literary Contest. He has published in the *Prairie Journal of Canadian Literature, Paragon Journal, The Nashwaak Review, NōD Magazine, White Wall Review, Echolocation, Wooden Rocket Press, The Broken City, Hart House Review,* and *Broken Pencil Death Match IV.*

Amy Stuart of Toronto is working on her first novel, and this summer will graduate with her M.F.A. in Creative Writing through UBC. In 2011 she was awarded the Writers' Union of Canada Short Prose Competition for Developing Writers.

Authors' Biographies

Phil Della of Vancouver, Washington, completed his Creative Writing degree at the University of Victoria. Now living in Maple Ridge, B.C., he is currently completing a youth mystery novel. He appeared in the UVic student journal, *Seventh Wave*, but this is his "first" publication.

Jacqueline Windh lives on Vancouver Island, and is a writer, photographer, and broadcaster. She is also a scientist, and uses her sciences background to bring a unique angle to her artistic works. She holds a B.Sc. and a Ph.D. in  Geology, and an M.F.A. in Creative Writing. Her first book, *The Wild Edge*, which she both wrote and photographed, is a Canadian best-seller. She is author or co-author of three other books, and her articles, stories, and photographs have been published in books, newspapers, and magazines both in Canada and internationally.

Kris Bertin works as a bartender and bouncer at Bearly's House of Blues and Ribs in Halifax. He has had stories published with the *Malahat Review, PRISM*, the *New Quarterly,* the *Antigonish Review, Riddle Fence, Pilot,* and others. He is from Lincoln, New Brunswick.

Martha Bátiz was born and raised in Mexico City, moved to Canada in 2003, and now lives in Richmond Hill, Ontario. Her articles, chronicles, reviews and short stories have appeared in newspapers and magazines in her  homeland, Spain, Dominican Republic, Puerto Rico, Peru, and Canada. Her first book was a collection of stories, *A todos* *los voy a matar* (*I'm Going to Kill Them All*). Her most recent work is the award-winning novella *The Wolf's Mouth* (Exile Editions; originally released in Spanish, both in the Dominican Republic and Mexico). She holds a Ph.D in Latin American Literature, is an ATA Certified Translator, offers a "Creative Writing in Spanish" course with the School of Continuing Studies at the University of Toronto, and is a part-time professor at York University/Glendon College.

Seán Virgo was born in Malta, and grew up in South Africa, Malaya, Ireland and the U.K.; he immigrated to Canada in 1966. He has published a dozen books of poetry and fiction; has won national magazine awards in both genres, as well as the CBC and the BBC competitions for short stories. In 2012 he will have two books published: *The Shadow Mother*, a story for "the almost children most of us are" which is illustrated by the Spanish artist Javier Serrano, and a collection of short fiction, *Dibidalen.* He is currently working on a novel.

AUTHOR WEBSITES/CONTACTS:
Christine Miscione ~ miscione.christine@gmail.com
Leon Rooke ~ www.leonrooke.com
Kelly Watt ~ www.kellywatt.ca
Darlene Madott ~ www.darlenemadott.com
Linda Rogers ~ www.lrogers.com
Daniel Perry ~ www.danielperryfiction.com
Amy Stuart ~ www.amystuart.ca
Phil Della ~ philmdella@gmail.com
Jacqueline Windh ~ www.jacquelinewindh.com
Kris Bertin ~ www.krisbertin.blogspot.ca
Martha Bátiz ~ marthabatiz@rogers.com
Seán Virgo ~ fidnemid@gmail.com

Prize Winners

Best Story by an Emerging Writer
↽ $3,000 ↼

Christine Miscione

Best Story by a Writer at Any Point of Career
↽ $2,000 Each ↼

Leon Rooke and Seán Virgo